robe of earth

A spiritual fantasy
Of the legendary
Mary of Magdala:

Book One

In the spirit of being who I really am.

by Flossie Jordan

DEDICATION

To St. Mary Magdalene.

Thank you for allowing me to put you in this role. It's probably as true as most other things written about you. Everything is fiction anyway.

IN APPRECIATION

With gratitude to those who have worked with me in this life: my parents, husband, brother, and sisters; friends and teachers who made me want a better way or helped me find one; all who taught me to enjoy my own company by rejecting me; those who enabled me find IT within myself; and persons who steered me the right direction by either putting obstacles in my path or opening the way. To individuals who played major roles in my life. Your performances have been brilliant and extremely believable. If we had known we were actors doing improvisational theatre, our performances would have been melodramatic and downright cheesy. But we didn't know, thanks to the veil of forgetfulness.

I appreciate the following for spiritual boosts: Catherine Greer, Ed Logan, Jim Jones, Joyce Reynolds, Ray Markley, and Sherryl Woodruff.

Thanks to Sasha Mabe, Roger Folyer, and Joseph Fields for encouraging this project.

To Janet Biery and others in Cookeville Creative Writers for listening to me read, to those who read my manuscript – Barbara Sandlin, Ralph Bowden, Joyce Sievers, Bill Kummer, Joan Kummer; to those who read proofs – Sara Hudgens, Danette Butson, Kelly Piepmeier, and Amy Anderson; to Arlene Dubo for my cover illustration and Patti Payne for graphic editing; and to Charlotte Seager for editing.

But most of all, to the unseen beings: Holy Spirit, God, sponsors, guardians, masters, angels, elementals who facilitate this sojourn. Your companionship lights my life. Your steadfast loyalty energizes me. Your ideas inspire. I couldn't do any of this without help from the higher frequencies..

Flossie Jordan

All the world's a stage, and all the men and women merely players: they have their exits and their entrances; and one man in his time plays many parts, his acts being seven ages.

William Shakespeare

As You Like It, Act II, Scene VII

Two thousand years to prepare.
Only two thousand years.
An enormous task requires unprecedented assistance.
By cosmic law, we cannot assist unless embodied humanity asks for help.
Our hands are tied.
The delegation sank deeper into the silence to listen to the wisdom of the ages.
We can take embodiment ourselves so that we can do the invocations.

SPIRITUAL HIERARCHY
HEAVEN

CONCLAVE TO PLAN
MISSION OF JESUS AND MARY OF MAGDALA
TO INITIATE THE AGE OF PISCES.

As Lord of the World, Sanat Kumara[1] was the presiding light. *came from Venus to save the Earth* The call to convene was written on the ethers of the Book of Life. Those interested in participating appeared simultaneously. All knew that Micah, Angel of Unity, was the master in charge of the spiritual dispensation for the next millennium of earth. They wondered who would embody the feminine aspect of deity to nurture and bring it into manifestation. Great beings of the sun, the brother and sister suns, and the sun behind the sun attended. Elohim and Elohae, the master builders of form for the Earth; Archangels and Archaii of divine feeling; and the Chohans of the Rays as well as their divine complements participated. There were many who had mastered their earthly energies and ascended including many who were still on the wheel of life and death on the school of Earth and sister planets. Elementals who were builders of form were eager to participate: the gnomes of the earth, the salamanders of the fire, the undines of the water, and the sylphs of the air.

All of heaven scintillated with anticipation of the Piscean age and expected to have a significant part in the drama of its inception. It would be notable enough to etch itself deeply on the annals of history and be sufficiently intriguing to be told over and over in the world of form.

---

[1] There is a list of characters, meaning of their names, and their relationships in the appendix.

Volunteers arrived in their etheric bodies. There was no need to take on human form in this gathering of light beings. When they appeared, they expanded their light to encompass the gathering and sat in the silence. (All absorbed themselves into the one mind, one mind in all, and shared their thoughts about the pageant they would mount on the stage of earth.)

Sanat Kumara directed the contemplation toward the needs of the hour. *Humankind must be prepared for freedom's dispensation at the end of the millennium. Therefore, they will need to learn responsibility and caring. Their consciousness of guilt and limitation must be set aside to let the Christ shine through their physical bodies. They will have to give up habits of thought that project shame and blame on to others, and (learn to extend divine thoughts and feelings to the screen of life.) Then they will be ready to accept freedom.*

The assembly responded with collective thoughts that reflected the possibilities for the planet's advancement.

Two thousand years to prepare.

Only two thousand years.

An enormous task requires unprecedented assistance.

By cosmic law, we cannot assist unless embodied humanity asks for help.

Our hands are tied.

The delegation sank deeper into the silence to listen to the wisdom of the ages.

We can take embodiment ourselves so that we can do the invocations.

Very dangerous.

We'll need extraordinary help to avoid taking on the destructive human effluvia that might hide our true thoughts and feelings from us.

The veil of illusion is almost impossible to overcome.

Those of us who embody should have an etheric sponsor who guides us. The guides can appear to us during sleep to keep us on task.

We can plan tribulations that will give us no choice but to fulfill our roles.

We'll need a special dispensation from the Karmic Board.

We work for the good of humanity. Surely it will be granted.

What kinds of roles will be needed?

First someone to teach the people to invoke the help we can give.

The religions do a passable job of this, but their prayers tend to be pedantic, mindless repetitions of prescribed prayers.

They need to engage their minds and pure feeling to give power to their prayers.

The religions are for priests. Common men involve themselves with mundane struggles for food, clothing, shelter, and defense. They don't know they can minister to each other and to themselves.

Empowering individuals to invoke us would increase our opportunities exponentially. Think what we could do if they consciously reach up to heaven.

The light bodies that we use here could expand from their central focus within the flesh body to unite with the spiritual hierarchy.

What great power humans have if they learn how to use it!

We must appear before the Karmic Board for permission to fill our lower bodies with the good of our Causal Bodies through the portal of our Holy Christ Selves.

Surely we can't be denied. Those with special missions are bestowed with special gifts for that embodiment.

The practice of meditation of the Buddhists needs to be shared with those in the Occident. They effectively set the example for the planet by reaching up to Heaven.

The Israelites in the Middle East brought forward ceremonial living. They have laws for every activity of life. This constant attention to the rules given them by Jehovah through Moses puts their thoughts on the name of God. That is a tremendous opportunity for our energy to enter the world of form. The Jewish yearn for a messiah to save them from oppression. We can use their longing as an open road to earthly consciousnesses.

The native people in the western hemisphere brought a remembrance of elemental life into the world. They communicate with nature and hold animals in great respect. They respond to the rhythms of heavenly bodies. the equinox and solstice of the sun, the new and full moon, the rotation of the earth.

The Greeks bring great intellect and recognition of our roles to step down God's vibration so it can be assimilated by humankind.

Unfortunately humankind has a tendency to exalt our celestial personalities and worship us as Gods and Goddesses.

When we point the way to the one true God, they feel small and don't think they can have a personal connection with such an infinite being. They don't understand how the vastness that is God could be interested in their small, insignificant self.

They must be made aware that the things they think they see are not real and what they think they think are not their true thoughts. This will give them the detachment they need to live in the silence even while experiencing monumental challenges. These need to be seen as only tests to move through.

The players in the pageant will set the example of how to live that will inspire humanity toward the consciousness they need for the next golden age.

We will embody to set the example.

The energy from one light-being expanded to command their consideration. The delegation grew still, emptied their thoughts, and attended to his. It was Micah, the great being in charge of the next dispensation. *I shall take embodiment to set the example of living as Christos in the world of form. People will see how I live and know how to put their Christhood into action through thought, feeling, word, and deed. I will be known as Jesus.*

The beings of light shimmered with enthusiasm as they raised their vibrations in anticipation, eager to be a part of the pageant that would launch the paradigm for the age.

The being who overshadowed the embodiment of Elijah took a place near Micah. *Humanity must expect the being that brings them the living Christos. I will be a harbinger for Jesus, the Christ to come. People will know that something special is about to happen. I will prepare the assistants. Those who embody to help Jesus will sojourn with me to safeguard their consciousnesses of responsibility. I will purify humanity so they can accept the new vibration. I will be called John, the Baptist.*

The Archaii of the fifth ray of truth, science, and healing joined Micah. *With my powers of concentration, I will hold the Immaculate Concept for your embodiment as Jesus, the messiah. I will nourish your fetus within the womb of my physical body and your growing character in the aura of my home. I will see you as Christos despite any evidence to the contrary. I will be your mother, Mary.*

Eleven others offered themselves as maidens who would bring children of promise into the world.

Archangel Gabriel would communicate with Mother Mary as a child and remind her of her mission at the proper time.

Saint Germain, Chohan of the seventh ray of transmutation and freedom joined Mother Mary. *I will be known as Joseph, Jesus' father. I will support you and Mary. I will take charge of your intellectual training and teach you a trade. I will chaperone when you go for spiritual training and stand firm to ensure we adhere to your true mission.*

There was a stirring in the crowd as volunteers rushed forward to claim the family positions. Six individuals in their light bodies took their places as Jesus' brothers and sisters. Another set rushed forward to be his friends. Others stepped forward to take places as followers and supporters.

The crowd was impressed as still others stepped forward to introduce conflict to the pageant: Herod, Pontius Pilate, Judas, and Caiphas. *Hey look! We said it had to be memorable.* There was a smattering of sardonic laughter.

The great masters of past ages came forward to pledge their inspiration and guidance during the embodiment. Mengste, Vidyapati, Kaspar, Ashbina, Apollo, Matheno, and Philo offered to embody as the Seven Sages of the World and meet with Jesus as Logos at strategic times during his bestowal for the earth.

El Morya, Chohan of the first ray, Kuthumi, Chohan of the second ray, and Dwahl Kuhl of the second ray stepped forward to be Hor, Lun, and Mer, Magi who would make humanity conscious that a great being was embodying.

Nada, who served as the Goddess of Love and the twin flame of Micah commanded the attention of all. *I will be your consort, Beloved Micah. I will hold you in my heart and assist you in your mission. I will model the divine feminine for humanity. I will teach the women in the entourage of the messiah. I will be named after Mary and begin my life in Magdala.*

She radiated her light to the crowd. And they stirred in excitement. It was a sign of the mission's importance for divine complements to embody together as partners.

Excitement built and Ascended Lady Kwan Yin, master of mercy, compassion, and exemplary family life stepped up to address Nada on the dais. *I will be your guardian and guide. I will appear in physical form to teach your embodied consciousness at auspicious times to propel your mission forward.*

A number of great beings stepped forward to assist Jesus and Mary Magdalene with the ministry. Archaii Faith of the first ray took the position of the disciple Peter. A great being of the sixth ray of devotion stepped forward as the disciple John. From the second ray of wisdom was James.

Serapis Bey, Chohan of the fourth ray, enthusiastically offered to teach Jesus and Mary Magdalene how to suspend the breath, resurrect their bodies, and ascend.

Lazarus was becoming adept in this area. *I'll be the human example to the world of being raised from the dead.*

Nada listed the qualities she needed for her mission: understanding, perseverance, discipline, tolerance, devotion to fulfilling her divine plan, hope, healing, truth, grace and ministration, compassion, peace, and enthusiasm. With Kwan Yin's help, the good of her causal body was more than enough to fulfill the purpose.

She sent forth a clarion call through the ethers. *Who will help me to assist Micah, Angel of Unity to birth the divine momentum for the Piscean Age?*

Master beings came at her call to be her supporters: Dora, her mentor; Enoch, her father; Dan, her brother; Leora and Sarina, her sisters; Deborah and Lizette, her friends; while Edita separated herself from the maidens around Mary to stand as Magdalena's mother.

Nada turned to a strong, unwavering light waiting to one side. *And what devious idea do you have in mind?*

I'll be Raamah, the first of your antagonists, the one who will make your childhood a living hell. He stepped aside to reveal another strong, but mischievous light. *This is my friend, Izaak. We will teach Magdalena to be strong.*

She agreed. *A terrible job, but someone has to do it.*

As if on cue, a group of friendly adversaries presented themselves as negative examples:

Nada was delighted. The entourage of light bubbled in laughter. She almost manifested a set of hands so she could rub them in glee. *Oh what a tangled web we weave when first we practice to deceive. Mary the Magdalene will have a strong character.*

Another contingent strived for recognition amid the enthusiasm. *We think Mary Magdalene will need friends.*

Raamah and the antagonists protested, *"We're her friends!"*

True, but you are negative examples. A human entity needs positive cohorts to keep from going crazy.

Dora proclaimed, *As your mentor, I'll help you understand what is happening.*

Edita announced, *I'll show you motherhood. I'll teach you far beyond the knowledge of other women and give you a sense of your role in history.*

Martha was practical, *I'll feed your helpers,* and her sister, Young Mary, said, *I'll be your student and show you appreciation.*

A cadre of spirits stepped forward to be Magdalene's students. Others were to become Holy Women and continue her teachings past her time.

I'll be Zadika. I'll be Raamah's mother and temper the effects of his machinations on you.

Nada could hardly keep from laughing. She looked at Raamah with affection. *I have a feeling that will be needed,* she replied to Zadika.

Zadika continued, *I'll be an altruistic example to you and show you the duties of an important man's wife.*

Eban stepped forward to be that important man. *I'll be the self-righteous priest of Magdala who will adhere to the letter of the law.*

Hannah exclaimed, *I'll help Zadika deceive this chauvinistic ruler of the synagogue.*

All those who would be women giggled conspiratorially. *We'll help you with that.*

Enough! Enough! All grew silent at Nada's bidding.

I love how clever you all are. You've taken roles for improvisation. We'll meet at important junctures in the life of Mary Magdalene and make specific adjustments as they are needed.

Now we'll go to Micah and coordinate our scripts with his group. They must fit together perfectly.

When the two casts came together, Micah took Nada aside and they watched as the plans moved along synergetically. Edita agreed to befriend Mother Mary as a young child. Andra, Diana, Josada, Margil, Miriam, Nanette, Sophi, Suzanna, Joanna, and Josie would each be one of twelve young maidens. They agreed to come to the Essene[1] community at Mount Carmel at an early age to train in the temple. The Archaii Constance of the second ray would embody as Judy to be their teacher. They planned where Jesus would be born and Margil would be midwife.

The wise men agreed to return to Jesus' life prior to the beginning of his ministry. The Oracle at Delphi would convert her following to him.

Sitting in his aura, Nada sensed what trials they planned for Jesus. With gratitude and understanding, they looked to those who would play the drama. Herod, Tiberius, Pontius Pilate, Judas, Peter, Roman Soldiers, Caiphas.

Nada marveled at the skill and ingenuity at play. *Let's hope they don't play their roles too well.*

---

[1] a sect living various cities. Some gathered to live a natural and simple communal life. They believed in oneness with God and prepared for the Piscean Age.

He nodded in agreement; *It's amazing that Master souls can concoct such devious drama.*

She concurred with an affectionate laugh. *I'm glad we trust them.*

They overlapped their auras to unite their oneness. *I'm glad we're in this together.*

They rested content, pleased with the divine potential of the pageant they were setting in motion.

And so the Piscean Age was launched. They planned their roles in meticulous detail, meeting together to coordinate their activities, refining their thought forms for the pageant to ensure its efficacy.

CHAPTER 1

Maggie stirred honey into the goat's milk. Her brother, Dan, came in and tousled her hair. "Good job with the milking."

She grinned up at him proudly. Dan was in his late adolescence and they expected him to form a family of his own soon. Then Maggie would take over his chores in the absence of other sons. Of the daughters, she was the most inclined to do the tasks usually assigned to boys. Her sisters were skillful workers, but the oldest, Leora, hadn't needed to do men's work because Dan, being close to her age, was there to do it. And Sarina was afraid of being kicked by a goat, pecked by a chicken, or butted by a ram, and she screamed at the sight of snakes and mice.

Their mother, Edita, had arranged the table assisted by Leora and Sarina. A hearty breakfast of bread, fish, apples, and chard was ready to eat. Their father, Enoch, came in from feeding the barnyard animals. He gave thanks to God as they broke bread.

Maggie and Dan were full of talk about Elsie. This was only Maggie's third time to milk Elsie and the goat was not yet willing to allow Maggie to touch her without Dan nearby. Elsie fondly butted Dan's leg to demand a few strokes from his strong, affectionate hand. Enoch hoped Elsie would transfer her affection to his youngest daughter. Maggie was good with animals, so things would probably go as planned.

Maggie loved her brother and he loved his littlest sister. He had carried her piggyback until she could walk fast enough to keep up. Now, he took her with him to tend the flock and Edita sighed as she watched them go. This was hardly the best pastime for a young girl. But what could they do? She had no other sons to help Enoch.

While the sheep safely grazed, they played catch, picked up rocks, or took turns pitching a ball and hitting it with a stick. Maggie learned to throw hard and hit a mark on the side of a hill. The sheep nonchalantly grazed and chewed their cud while lambs alternately played and suckled the ewes. Dan and Maggie's activities no longer fazed them.

Dan carried a slingshot to protect the sheep from predators. Maggie enthusiastically learned to swing it for momentum so she could surprise prey with an accurate hurl.

Dan and Maggie sat in front of a cave on the shady side of the hill with a panoramic view of the countryside and the grazing flock. Dan improvised melodies on his flute and Maggie sang songs to calm the herd. Their well trained dogs positioned themselves on the other side of the sheep, Bo at one end and Abbe at the other. They circled the herd calmly, ran after stray lambs, and coaxed them back to the flock. They were trained to bark ferociously to scare away predators, alerting Dan of the danger at the same time.

This was a fair spring day and bees floated lazily above sage blossoms whose subtle fragrance perfumed the air. Some ewes still carried their lambs while others were already born. Dan was alert for more lambing.

Maggie and Dan threw the ball to each other. She was proud that he was one of the better players in the evening stickball games. She loved to walk with him to his games and hold his stick until it was his turn to hit the ball. The game depended on Dan who was the most important player because he was most often chosen to pitch.

Dan taught Maggie to throw. He went easy on her until she was six, but now that she was ten he threw her the ball with the same force he used with his teammates. She bested him when she could. They threw their balls at marks drawn on the side of the hill. When thrown straight and true, balls rolled directly back to them and they didn't have to retrieve them.

Maggie went on alert. The sheep stopped grazing, their heads up, and their ears all pointing toward the outcropping of rock. There was danger there. "Dan!"

As he turned to check, Bo and Abbe raced toward the cave on the south side of the hill behind the rock.

"Calm the flock," Dan commanded as he hurried toward the dogs with his sling.

Bessie, the old ewe, quickened her steps. If Maggie didn't stop her before she ran, the sheep would scatter across the countryside in fright. Maggie grabbed her harp and sang a lovely song while she slowly walked toward Bessie, the head of the flock, the one the other sheep would follow. She comforted her and led her away from the barking dogs while Dan stalked the predator. She kept her voice calm, subtly quickened the tempo, and added a walking rhythm on the harp. Maggie serenely checked the rear for straggling lambs and the sides for rovers. She led Bessie toward a stray until the lamb sighted his kind and ran back.

"Heel!" The barking subsided at Dan's call and Maggie circled back toward Dan, continuing to play and sing. He soon emerged from behind the rocks with a lamb in his arms. The dogs followed, their heads hanging low.

As he came closer, her heart fell. Was the lamb dead or only injured? She looked at Dan with a question in her eyes.

Its bloody body struggled to breathe, jugular vein throbbing. She let her harp hang behind her back and took the young lamb from Dan. "What was it?"

"A jackal. I'll tell you about it this evening. Go home and mend its wounds. I'll finish the day with the flock. Take Abbe with you."

Dan could have used both dogs, but Maggie, being a young female, needed protection.

She put a cloth on the injury to stop its bleeding and briskly carried the wounded, frightened lamb. Abbe whimpered in concern at her side, hurrying, and leaping upward to see if the lamb was all right. Maggie paused to pat the dog's head over its worried eyes. "The baby will be fine. We'll take her to Dora." She lifted the cloth to check the bleeding. Dora was the local healer. Luckily, her hut was on the way into town.

She entered the dwelling, saw Dora wasn't there, and placed the lamb on the table. Maggie felt at home here, having helped Dora since she was young. Abbe sat on her haunches looking up at the lamb. Her eyes followed Maggie as she soaked a rag in water and washed the wound. She made a salve of camphor and gently spread it over the area. She soothed the lamb and waited for it to calm. The dog settled, relaxed but alert, her muzzle between her extended paws. Nevertheless her eyes were open wide with ears perked and a frown marred her forehead. Occasionally a worried whine escaped her throat.

Maggie smiled affectionately and reached out her hand. Abbe nuzzled Maggie and received some head strokes, her tail wagging and thumping the floor.

Maggie sang and caressed the lamb. The dog lost interest in being petted and curled at her feet. The lamb's breathing slowed until it slumbered peacefully. Maggie left them to go outside and tend the garden for Dora. She pulled some weeds and dead-headed some flowers while the events of the morning replayed in her head. She gathered some herbs and took them inside to separate the leaves from the stalks and put them in a basket to dry. She then put dry leaves in a mortar, and used a pestle to grind them into a powdery tea.

When the lamb stirred, Maggie placed a milk-soaked cloth inside a roll of leather to form a teat. She tilted it toward the lamb's mouth who suckled hungrily. "Rafaela, God has healed. I'm going to call you Rafaela, beloved one," she said decisively and set the milk aside and fondled her tenderly.

Dora came in, tired from tending a birth and, seeing how neat everything was, she sank gratefully into a chair, "I see you've finished the work I was doing."

"I used it to pass the time while watching that lamb heal."

Dora's eyes widened, "Injured? Sick?"

"Attacked and mutilated by a jackal." She told Dora all she knew. "I don't know if Dan got the culprit. I'll learn more at supper after the flock comes in. I used your camphor to make a poultice and fed Rafaela some of your sheep's milk."

Dora absently rubbed Abbe's back. "You're welcome to it, honey. You did my day's work. Now all I have to do is lie down to sleep. It's been a long two days."

"I'd best be going. Mom's started supper and the men will be in soon."

"God bless you."

Edita saw Maggie come into the yard with Abbe. When she spotted the injured lamb, she dropped her dish towel and ran to her. "What happened?"

Maggie told about the jackal, calming the flock, and stopping by Dora's. Dan arrived with the flock. Though anxious to hear Dan's side of the story, Edita instructed, "Feed the dogs and settle the animals for the night. We'll hear more about this later."

Maggie washed while Sarina and Leora prepared supper. Enoch arrived followed by Dan. They took their helpings after the blessing. Conversation centered on the events in the pasture, with both Maggie and Dan telling parts of the story. They complimented Dan for stunning the jackal and slitting its throat. Leora gladly accepted the jackal's pelt. She would make a drinking vessel of it.

When Maggie told of carrying the lamb to Dora's with only a dog to protect her, Enoch and Edita silently flashed their concern, but knew it couldn't be helped. Maggie's resourcefulness pleased them. She was capable and confident to be so young.

Maggie played games with the boys in the village when she could. She rarely sat on the sidelines and watched with the other girls. When she ran errands, she often wore Dan's striped robes and played stickball with the boys rather than wearing bright girlish capes with colorful sashes. She wasn't particularly attractive. She scoffed at Leora and Sarina's ideas of feminine allure and made fun when they dressed to please, pinched their cheeks to make them rosy, and stained their lips with berries. They sat on the sidelines to encourage the boys and vied for their attention during games.

Maggie cheered Dan and his best friend, Samuel. She played for the first time when Dan needed one more teammate. She played so well that the boys were glad to have her.

On the day she met Jesus, he played on the opposite team.

She wasn't supposed to play that day, but when she went to the well for water, she saw the game start, couldn't resist, and put down her urn.

She took the ball and walked across from the hitter. She assessed the new boy holding the stick across from her. He was taller than the others with a disarming smile and dancing eyes. He got into position with a big grin across his face. He sized her up and readied to hit the ball. She crouched forward, aimed, took a step back, and powerfully propelled the ball across the plate. His stick sent it down the street and Maggie's team chased it. She caught the ball from Tobias and threw it to a baseman while the boy ran. Judging from the great distance of his hit, he would make it around the bases. With perfect timing she blocked him, slammed to the ground, and felt his weight fall on top of her.

~Ouch!~ That would teach her to watch where she was going.

Thinking he should score after such a long hit, he scrambled to finish his run.

Maggie rushed to help her teammates tag him out. Yaar caught the ball after a bounce, threw it to Enosh who passed it to Maggie who had beaten the runner to third base. She caught it just before he slid into the plate.

The new boy flicked dust from his tunic, "Good play. I'm impressed. I felt sure I had that one." She winced as he shook her hand. "Are you okay?" he asked.

"Yes, I've fallen down before. No big deal. You're not that heavy."

"But you're hurt." She flinched as he started to pull her up by her hands. He hesitated and turned them over, "Your hands are scraped and bleeding. Let me help you with that. He led her to the well. "Stay here."

She shook the dust off her garb and absently watched the game go on without them. He detached the wooden pail from the cistern and washed the grime off her wounds. Still shaken from the blow and disarmed by his nearness, she gathered her wits about her, "Thank you."

He sat on the wall beside her and looked at her with interest, "Do you come here every day?"

She responded gratefully, glad to take her mind off her fall. "I come three times a day to get water. I haven't seen you before. Are you new to Magdala or just visiting?"

"I'm here from Nazareth with my father. He's a carpenter and we're building a new home on the edge of town. I play stickball with the boys before supper."

She looked over at the boys playing. The ball rolled over to the well beside her water vessel. "The jar! Oh! I almost forgot." She remembered why she was there and knew that her mother needed water soon. Getting ahead of her, he placed the sturdy pot on the edge of the well. She held it steady while he lowered the pail into the water.

He smiled at her with friendly eyes, "I'm Jesus. Do you live around here?"

She pointed down a side street, "I live over by that hill."

"I'll see you around. We'll be in town for a while."

"I'm Maggie. Thank you for rescuing me from my wounds."

She balanced the urn on her head walked home. ~Jesus.~ She sighed dreamily remembering his merry eyes and kindness. He was nicer than other boys who found games more important than helping someone. They didn't even know she was a girl. She wondered if he would be at the well tomorrow. How thoughtful of him to stop playing to help her! She tried to think of other boys who might respond to her predicament, but they were so absorbed in the game that her dilemma went unnoticed. Of course, her presence was not unusual to them. ~And he even knew to wash the wound,~ she thought

Pleasure swelled at the thought of sitting with him on the wall by the well and his gentle touch as he checked for wounds. He was more attractive than the neighbor boys and better at stickball. He enjoyed every minute of the game.

She turned at the gate and chickens scurried out of her way as she entered the house by the side door. In the kitchen Mother, Leora, and Sarina prepared the evening meal. She placed the water vessel on the high counter. "Does anybody know who's building a new home on the edge of town?" she asked.

Mother sent a significant glance to Leora. "Do you want to tell her or shall I?"

"Let's wait until supper when everyone's at the table." Leora put the cake on the table to cool while she mixed a glaze to pour over it.

"We're having cake," Maggie said. "That's special. Are we having company?" She loved to have people come over.

"Yes, set the table for thirteen. It's a surprise." Mother stirred a pot of vegetables and sliced the bread.

Maggie ran her hand over the smooth texture of the pottery as she put out the plates. Her father, Enoch, was a talented potter and his children learned his craft. Leora, the oldest, had almost completed a set of dishes for her hope chest. Sarina had already made a decent start on hers, and Maggie knew that she would someday make a set for herself.

Her thoughts returned to the supper surprise. Why didn't they tell her who was building the new house? She guessed it was for someone they knew. Otherwise, it wouldn't be important enough to be a surprise. ~Who are we honoring with cake? I wonder who's coming over?~

Filling the goblets with water, she thought again of the friendly stranger who filled her jar at the cistern. She hoped she would see him again tomorrow.

She heard a rumble of voices and footsteps down the lane. Edita wiped her hands with a damp towel and opened the front door wide. Enoch strode into the house, pecked her cheek, and welcomed the guests behind him. Their friends, Jonathan and Nanette were followed by their three children, Samuel, Janette, and Deborah. Dan brought up the rear. Squealing, Maggie ran to Deborah, took her hand, and they sat together on the far side of the table. This was indeed a nice surprise.

Samuel held up a basket of fish. "With compliments to the hostess," he said and Sarina took them to the counter before joining her friend, Janette, at the long table. Enoch and Edita took their places at the ends. Leora and Dan sat on the side near the kitchen and Maggie was surprised to see that Samuel took the place on the other side of Leora. Samuel and Dan usually sat together because they were buddies. She wondered who would sit at the two extra places across from her.

From the head of the table, Enoch announced, "Go ahead and serve the fruit. Jonathan's brother-in-law and nephew will be here soon. They had to stop by the carpenter shop on the way."

Edita passed the bowl to Maggie. The conversation turned to Jonathan and Samuel's catch of the day. The Sea of Galilee was a fisherman's dream, enabling them to fill their nets in early morning and spend the day at the market. Samuel saved the best for Edita, knowing he would have dinner with her family.

Someone knocked before they finished the fruit. Dan opened the door for the two other guests. Maggie gasped in surprise to see the boy behind his father. Enoch stood to shake their hands and introduce them, "This is Joseph and his son, Jesus." The new guests sat across from Maggie.

Jesus was as surprised and pleased to see Maggie as she was to see him. His eyes riveted on hers as the fruit came his way. Holding the bowl, Dan waited for Jesus to take it and raised his eyebrows in amusement when he noticed their guest staring across the table at

Maggie. Dan discretely cleared his throat and Jesus hurriedly took the dish and helped himself to a sprig of grapes.

Dan watched the two thoughtfully. His youngest sister was growing up and this talented and energetic boy was attracted to her. He would watch out for his little sister. In two short years, she would be bat mitzvah[1]. He took a serving of fish.

He was never concerned about Leora. He and Leora were near the same age and played with Samuel as long as he could remember. Lately, Samuel and Leora took a different kind of interest in one another. Samuel would be part of the family.

Samuel's cousin, Jesus, likely possessed similar character. Dan decided to make his acquaintance, especially if he was interested in Maggie.

Edita put clean goblets before each guest and Enoch poured. Returning to the head of the table, he rang with his spoon. "It gives me great pleasure to announce that Samuel has asked for Leora's hand in marriage. Her mother and I approve of this match. Let's drink a toast to the happy couple." They each raised their glasses and sipped the wine.

Jonathan stood, "As father of the groom, I wish to announce that we are building a house next to ours for Samuel and Leora. My sister's husband, Joseph, is here to supervise the carpenters."

Dan raised his glass, "This calls for another sip of wine."

Now that the secret was out, everyone talked at once.

Maggie said to Jesus, "You didn't tell me you were kin to Deborah."

"I didn't know you were friends. Since my cousin and your sister are to be married, I'll see you when I visit Samuel and Leora."

"Sure. You're helping to build their house. Do you help your father with everything or do you have a special task?"

"Father lets me do more now. At first, I ran errands and fetched supplies. Now, I do whatever no one else is doing. If the other help is unskilled, I help Father set up jobs and do finish work. If we're working with journeymen carpenters, I assist."

"What can Deborah and I do to help with Leora's house?"

"I think you'll help a lot." He looked over where the two mothers talked. "Edita and Nanette will tell you what to do. Since your family does pottery, you'll probably make the sink. You'll make

---

[1] daughters' coming of age ritual.

lace valances, weave curtains, and bring food and water to the carpenters. There are jobs for everyone."

"Maggie, we'll help with the wedding too," Deborah said. "We'll arrange flowers for Samuel and Leora's arbor."

Maggie loved all things associated with gardening: working the soil, planting the seeds, watering, and deadheading the blooms. She even enjoyed picking fruit and vegetables and preserving them. She was excited about the wedding.

CHAPTER 2

Dora's little dwelling was surrounded by numerous plants to make herbal concoctions. As Maggie approached, she smelled boiling dandelion leaves. Dora steeped them into a strong tea for digestion. Jars of dried herbs filled shelves on one wall. The table was piled high with ginger root to be made into a poultice for breathing disorders.

"I'm glad you're here." She gave Maggie a spoon to stir the pot.

"I brought you a loaf of bread and some fish from last night's supper," Maggie said. "Leora and Samuel are getting married and they're building a house beside Jonathan and Nanette. Samuel brought us a string of fish, so we have plenty."

Dora nodded knowingly, "I'm not surprised. Their marriage will simply be a continuation of their lives."

"They're getting married when the house is built. Jonathan's brother-in-law, Joseph of Nazareth, is here to build the home. His son, Jesus, came with him. His mother stayed home with his brothers and sisters."

"Hmmm. How old is Jesus?"

"I guess he's eleven. I don't think he's bar mitzvah[1]."

"He's a year older than you."

"What are you thinking, Dora? You don't think I'll be a match for Jesus?"

"Who am I to say? Stranger things have happened. You just follow your instincts, dear. Your life will unfold according to your destiny." She chopped the roots with her knife. "Tell me about Jesus."

Maggie stirred the pot thoughtfully, "He's friendly . . . and thoughtful. He helped me when I fell playing stickball. Oh. And you'll like this. He knows about healing."

---

[1] sons' coming of age ritual.

"Hmmm. A young man who knows about healing. He must be very special."

"I'm excited about Leora and Samuel's wedding." Maggie confided things to Dora she wouldn't tell her mother, sisters, or best friend. Dora's wisdom and detachment from the ups and downs of life made Maggie feel safe. She wouldn't judge her or push Maggie to fulfill her own expectations. She loved Maggie with the unconditional love given one's own child.

From the time when Maggie came to fetch herbs as a young child, she had a special interest in the healing arts. This endeared her to Dora and made them kindred spirits. Dora was a sympathetic listener who kept Maggie's childish notions alive. Maggie listened when Dora said that something would point her to a wondrous purpose.

Maggie's mother tried to teach her to humble herself, never put herself forward, to wait to be asked, wait in line, and graciously let others go first. Those lessons were more effective for Sarina than for Maggie. Edita also said she could do anything she wanted to do and be anything she wanted to be. She need only believe in herself and try. Her father, Enoch, taught her not to expect too much so that she wouldn't be disappointed if things didn't go her way.

But Dora taught her that she was so much more than she could possibly imagine, that the spirit of God in her was her divine reality. She encouraged her to look beyond appearances and accept everything life has to offer with joy and enthusiasm.

Maggie's tomboyish ways amused Enoch and Edita. They were proud when she outran all the boys and pitched in the neighborhood stickball games. It amazed them that she also danced with the girls and sang beautifully at synagogue. They were delighted that Dora took her as an apprentice. Though considered eccentric by many, Dora was a good woman who loved their daughter and gave her something they could never give her.

Maggie was motivated by the feeling that she would do something special with her life. Her experiences led to something although she didn't know what that was or where it might lead. Time would tell. Each moment was a special anticipation that led to the next. What a glorious circle life was! It continually spiraled upward.

Dora encouraged her to analyze her experiences, observe whether they were in line with her dreams, and let her mind expect what she truly wanted. She created her own world according to her intentions.

This was directly opposite from what Enoch led her to believe. He expected her to live up to others' expectations, but she was determined not to accept less than she wanted.

She was aware that her friends and sisters did not know what they wanted. They imagined their lives would be like their parents. As a result, life happened to them based on their reactions to external circumstances that they judged joyous or disappointing. They chose from what they perceived in their environment. They thought that Leora and Samuel's friendship followed by an inevitable betrothal looked good. Therefore, they wanted something similar. They expected something like their parents' nice house with four children, animals, a pottery business, and regular visits to the synagogue. That was the way it was. It wouldn't occur to them to presume differently.

They thought it was fine to sit in the women's section at synagogue, for men to be the teachers and assume all the leadership roles, for the man to rule the household, to arrange marriages, preside at the table, and carve the meat.

Maggie wouldn't judge others for their own sincere ways of being. If you compare yourself to others, you're destined to be like them. She understood this and wasn't having any of it. She would make her own world.

Today, Dan worked on Samuel and Leora's house and Enoch went to the field so that Maggie could spend time reading from the Bible with Edita and the other girls. Girls from other families did not learn to read. They thought reading was only for men. Enoch and Edita didn't agree and had taught Leora with Dan since the two of them were close to the same age. Sarina learned when she was ready and Maggie learned with her.

Today, they read of Ruth and Naomi. Maggie was glad that the story of Ruth was in the Bible. It had no spiritual message, but told how Ruth came to live in Bethlehem and became the great-grandmother of King David. The love and loyalty between Ruth and Naomi was remarkable. It demonstrated that relatives were not always the strongest relationships. Naomi's love motivated her to release her daughters-in-law to return to the embrace of their birth families to seek their own destinies apart from her. Then when Ruth insisted on staying with Naomi, she rejoiced in Ruth's love, nourished it, and sought what was best for the daughter of her heart. She cleverly used her deceased husband's blood ties to finesse Ruth's marriage to Boaz. And Ruth was equally crafty in seeing it through.

They were poor and destitute because Naomi's husband and sons died. Ruth had no children, so Naomi sent her to glean in the fields of Boaz among other work-women. Ruth worked diligently from morning to night.

"Mother, why did Boaz tell his men not to molest her? Were they in the habit of bothering women?" Maggie asked.

Edita didn't mind, for Maggie read ahead. She was about to ask some crucial questions about men and women and possibly sex. Maggie was old enough to have them answered.

"Probably not, but some men do. A few might follow along to avoid losing face. Still others wouldn't harass a woman no matter what, but they fear retaliation if they hinder those who do. Luckily, there are few lecherous men. Tradition compels men to respect women. The men in our family protect us. No one would bother you when you are with Dan or Enoch. They know they would be avenged without hesitation."

"Why should men protect us? Why can't we just protect ourselves?"

Leora and Sarina frowned uncomfortably and Edita smiled at Maggie's naiveté. Her older daughters would not ask such a question.

"They are stronger than we are," Leora said as a matter of fact.

Sarina agreed, "They can hold us down and knock us unconscious."

Maggie was adamant, "We're smarter than they are and we can outsmart them."

"You would have to be very clever," Edita warned. "If you knew someone was going to attack you, you could distract him, appeal to his vanity, or fool him into thinking you'll submit to him until you see a way to escape. Then you'd have to run and hide."

"Mother, have you ever had to defend yourself like that?"

"Not really. My brothers sometimes tried to get back at me for taunting them or punish me for hiding from them at the market, but I was never really in danger. But, I tricked them into letting me go."

"Mother," Maggie hesitated because she wasn't sure Edita would answer her next question. Heretofore, such queries were neatly sidestepped, or ignored.

Edita waited expectantly, "Yes, Maggie."

Maggie took a breath and plunged in, "Did Boaz think that those men might hurt Ruth?"

"He knew it was a possibility. That's the reason he charged the reapers not to molest her. To avoid her attracting the attention of men, he also told her to keep her eye on the field and stay with the other work-women. The lesson in that is not to ask for trouble. Another important principle is to give and expect respect and you will get it."

Sarina added, "Boaz was a generous man. He appreciated Ruth's devotion to Naomi and made her way easier because of it. He made sure that she had water, bread, and wine and gave her extra barley."

"Naomi sent Ruth to Boaz's field because she was protected there," Leora put in.

"She also saw opportunity in the situation and told Ruth how to maximize her options," Maggie speculated. "She bathed, perfumed herself, and dressed up."

"That is the way women attract men," Edita said. "Ruth was obvious and Boaz clearly understood her message when she lay at his feet and told him to cover her. He agreed to do his duty as next of kin."

"Does that mean they made love?" Leora asked.

"I don't know for sure, but he asked her to stay the night and filled her mantle with barley for Naomi the next morning."

Sarina was logical, "They couldn't have made love. They are in the Bible so they must have been chaste. They weren't married."

"But in those days, men could have more than one wife," Maggie remembered, "and concubines. Solomon had thousands and was deemed holy enough to build the Temple."

"But women kept themselves for one man, even if that man had many women," Leora reminded.

"That's not fair," Maggie said indignantly.

"Not if it is desirable for a man to complicate his life with many wives and children," Edita responded. "Solomon was a king, so polygamy was a sign of power and commanded respect. In Jacob's time, it took many wives and children to tend animals and do farm work."

"I wouldn't want to share my husband."

"Neither would I." said Leora.

"Me neither." Sarina agreed.

That afternoon, Maggie went to Dora's hut with bread and vegetables. She stirred a concoction while Dora measured herbal blends for various illnesses.

"Dora, my sisters and I aren't allowed to go anywhere alone, yet you live by yourself and go out to tend the sick. Don't you need the protection of a man?"

"It's true I often travel alone, but I am older and not very attractive to men. I think they respect my medicine bag. I'm detached from things that do not concern me. The idea of a healer being accosted is foreign to me. I expect to be safe.

"Also, someone usually is with me when I go out at night. Night calls are emergencies and a messenger fetches me and accompanies me to the location. I'm often alone on daily rounds, when I deliver medicines, or sit in the market selling scented oils.

"Sometimes someone goes with me to keep me company." She smiled at Maggie. "Thank you."

Maggie sipped her own tea and gave a mug to Dora.

"What brings this up?" Dora asked. "Are you thinking of traveling?"

"We read the story of Ruth this morning."

"Oh," Dora nodded knowingly.

"Do you think Ruth and Boaz had sex?"

"Of course they did. They were the great-grandparents of David."

"I mean when she spent the night with Boaz on the threshing floor."

"Does it say they had sex?"

"No, but it does say she lay at his feet until morning. And he said 'It must not be known that this woman came to the threshing floor.' He kept it secret. He made sure that she left before the sun was up so that she wouldn't be recognized. So maybe they didn't do anything, but he arranged his marriage to her the next day."

"Well, it's true that when adults say 'sleep together,' it is a euphemism for having sex. What difference does it make?"

Maggie considered this. "It's in the Bible. That sets them up as examples for us to follow. Naomi and Ruth were manipulative. They trapped Boaz into marriage and Ruth may have had sex with a man outside of marriage."

"I see." Dora packed her concoctions in her medicine bag. "We'll never know for sure. The story was different for each telling until someone finally wrote it down. It was told for centuries. Storytellers embellished and took away depending on the time, the audience, and their own whims. I think you can decide for yourself." She put her hand on Maggie's, "It doesn't matter."

"Why not?"

"Going by rules and examples will only get you so far. Few things are cut and dried. When it really matters, you will follow your own heart and do what you think is best. Your inherent goodness ensures that you use your life rightly."

"Ruth didn't follow her own heart. She did what Naomi told her and we are to believe everything happened as it was supposed to happen."

"Some people depend on advisors. You can be one of those if you want."

"So, I have a choice, to follow my own heart, go by the laws and rules, or follow the example and advice of others?"

"Yes, you get to decide. Just remember that your heart may show you that the rules, examples, and experience can be applicable to certain situations, but not all."

They left the hut and walked down the road to make deliveries.

"Why do women try so hard to attract men? Ruth dressed up to attract Boaz and he was sweaty and covered with barley dust from winnowing on the chaffing floor."

"Ruth had a lot to gain by attracting him. She needed him to see her as an attractive woman. Before, he only saw her in working clothes and thought she was just another maiden gleaning in the field."

"That's true! He didn't recognize her when she came to him in all her finery. He said 'Who are you?' Okay," Maggie conceded, "I agree that Ruth had reason to primp that day. I just think that we don't need a man to make our way in the world. Look at you."

"I am very fortunate. I continued doing what I do until everyone expected it."

"There's a special category for you."

"And I like that, but don't forget that I accept help when it is offered. My patients help me and give me things in gratitude for my services. As I give healing, God pours it through me so that I'm seldom sick. Those who are healed return energy to me. They receive healing because they accept healing. Giving is receiving."

"That may be the most important lesson of your life."

"Maggie you are wise beyond your years. You make me happy to be who I am."

Enoch needed Dan to help plow the garden and Leora went with Maggie to graze the sheep. They packed a lunch and Maggie took her harp. Leora wouldn't play stickball with her, and Maggie didn't want her to. She threw like a girl, but she danced like a gazelle. They opened the gate for the flock. Maggie led while Abbe and Bo took their positions at the back and side of the herd with Leora on the other side.

On the way they met Samuel and Jesus. Samuel gave Leora flirting glances and invited her to the market to find things for their home. Jesus offered to take Leora's place with the sheep.

It didn't matter to Maggie who went with her. She felt capable of tending the sheep alone.

Jesus fell in beside her. All right. She liked Jesus and thought it would be fun to be with him. She guessed he felt the same or he wouldn't offer to spend the day with her.

"I thought you would be fishing with your Uncle Jonathan today."

"He's helping Father so I'm not needed. I'm ahead with the supplies, so I went to the market with Samuel. I don't think he expected to see Leora."

"You're right, she usually helps Mother with housework, but today, Dan was needed in the garden and they won't allow me to go to the pasture alone. She seldom goes with the sheep."

He grinned, "I understand that Samuel would rather have Leora with him than me."

"I think they're really in love," Maggie said. "If I ever get married, I hope it's a love match."

She released a breath. She had shocked herself. What a thing to say to a boy she had just met! Or any boy for that matter. But Jesus didn't seem to think it odd. He might be another girl or any other confidante. "Me too. I don't think everyone should get married. Some people have other callings."

"Like Dora."

They continued their walk beside the flock.

"Jesus, do you think that it's okay for a woman not to get married?"

"Of course, but women have few other options in our culture. They are considered loose if they go out alone. But men, even boys, have more choices, more freedom. For example, you wanted to tend the sheep alone today. You knew it wouldn't be allowed so you didn't even ask. But look at you! Deuteronomy states that it's an abomination for women to dress in men's clothes, and you're doing it."

Maggie laughed, "And I haven't been stoned. Wonder how much longer I can get by with it." She was unsettled that he already knew her so well, but sensed that she could talk to him about anything. Maybe it would be a good day after all.

"Tell me about Dora."

"She's our local wise woman who heals the sick and attends births. She lives alone and goes by herself on deliveries and sick calls."

"You admire her, don't you?"

"Very much. She's a good friend."

"I think it's important to know adults that are not relatives to expand our field of reference. It's nice that you have Dora. Most girls don't have outside mentors."

"But boys go to school where there are many teachers. Do you have teachers who are special to you, Jesus?"

"Rabbi Barachia at my school in Nazareth is open-minded and listens to my ideas. He interprets the Torah in a traditional way to keep the approval of the elders, but a few of us know that he has an expanded viewpoint. We love to ponder other ideas and discuss deeper matters than the Law. He trusts us and knows he can be more open with us."

"How can you miss school in Nazareth? Are you teacher's favorite?"

He laughed easily, "Not really. I challenge the chazzan[1] and ask too many questions to be his favorite. I am allowed to miss school for one week of every month because I stay ahead of the class."

"So you help Joseph that week?"

"Sometimes. I often stay at my Uncle Jeremiah's farm south of Nazareth or come here to fish with Uncle Jonathan and Samuel. I want to experience all walks of life."

"Why?"

"So I can understand and help them."

Wow. A boy who wasn't out for himself and who wanted to help people. Was this possible?

They walked peacefully, checking the flock. The dogs did their job efficiently. They reached a field just beyond yesterday's, giving it a chance to recover from the close grazing of the day before.

"I see you brought your harp. Are we going to sing to the sheep?"

"I brought it today because Leora likes to dance. When I come with Dan, we play catch and throw the ball against a hill. Do you like to sing?"

They sat in the shadow of an olive tree and she tentatively strummed her harp sending rich harmonies echoing across the valley. She sang of the sun, water, air, and earth.

He listened to her elegant tones, pure and compelling. The sheep ceased their grazing and stared transfixed at the source of the sound. He had never heard such haunting beauty. At its end, he released the breath he was holding with an appreciative sigh. It was a moment before the sheep continued to graze. The dogs wagged their tails happily.

Fascinated by her, he looked into her eyes, took her hand, and held it between his, then lifted it to his lips for an appreciative kiss. "I have never heard anything so pure and lovely."

She shuddered with pleasure she had never experienced. What was that unfathomable calm that overcame her like sinking deep into a well? In her heightened awareness the call of the birds was enhanced, the sound more pronounced as the sheep tore clover from its stalks, the eyes of the dogs were brighter as they moved over the flock. The grass pushed through the fertile soil, and butterflies played at their pastime of flying in winding paths over wild daisies. Birds

---

[1] cantor or person who leads songful prayer

settled in the tree above the two shepherds and bold butterflies rested on her head offering to be her crown.

They sat in silence, comfortable in the tranquil spell she conjured with her song.

Jesus held the fragile silence knowing that once they spoke, the mood would be broken and it was ever so pleasant. But he had questions, "How do you know that song? It's not in Psalms."

She was reluctant to reveal her source, for it was from a little known spiritual group whose views had sparked controversy in the synagogues.

"Do you know it?"

"Yes."

"Then you know where it came from. How do you know it?"

He sensed that he was talking to a kindred spirit.

"My Father is part of the Essene fellowship and I have relatives in Hebron, in the hills of Judah; Elizabeth, and her son, John."

She sighed in relief, "My father and mother met when they were studying with the Essenes. I learned the song from them. I like these songs better than the Psalms. So many Psalms assume we are terrible sinners and that our enemies are smote by God."

"I agree. I don't like the idea that a people is chosen by a God who excludes everyone else and advocates war."

"Or one that punishes people."

"Or makes unreasonable laws."

It was so refreshing to talk to another initiate that she articulated her belief about God. "I believe that God is a loving light being and we are copies of his light. Even Genesis says we are made in his image. God is unseen by human eyes, but we feel Him in our soul without being seen or heard."

"Like now, Maggie. You invoked that into the world with your song. That peace we feel is the presence and love of God."

He stood and pulled her to her feet. Ecstatic that they found each other, they ran, laughing, to the center of the field, and holding hands, spun around in a circle until they were dizzy and fell onto a soft cushion of wildflowers. Breathless, they rolled onto their backs, breathing heavily until they recovered. They reached out to each other to clasp hands.

"Maggie, are there other Essenes in Magdala?"

"None, except your uncle and aunt. Father and Mother have friends who nod in agreement when they express their views, but none have asked the right questions to learn the precepts. We live our creed quietly without criticizing the teachings of the synagogue and we participate in traditional rituals. We live in the community though we are not of it."

"So there are only two families that you know about."

"Yes, and we think that Samuel and Leora must have a divine calling because their marriage will unite our families. Theirs will be an Essene family."

Jesus and Maggie left the harp and their lunch in a cool cave and strolled around the sheep. Maggie was gratified to see Rafaela cavorting with the other lambs and she told Jesus of Rafaela's rescue from the jackal.

They ate lunch by the cave and took another walk around the flock singing Essene songs. Maggie played a gathering song on her harp as she approached Bessie, the ewe who would lead them back to the pen for the night. As usual, Bo and Abbe took the rear. What a blessing it was to have well trained animals!

CHAPTER 3

Maggie took Jesus to Dora's hut the next day with mushrooms they had gathered from the mouth of a cave. "Dora not only heals, her wisdom is beyond that of the Essene Brotherhood. She delves into spiritual realities and thinks outside the realm of earthly possibilities."

She knew Dora would enjoy having Jesus in her home. He was different from other young people who were obsessed with stickball and attracting the opposite sex. She thought there would be a lively interaction between Jesus and Dora.

When they arrived, Dora was sitting on her front patio clipping roots in a comfortable chair. She seemed to expect them. They worked with her basket of eucalyptus.

Dora was talkative, "It's wonderful that nature provides sustenance and healing. Nature spirits consecrate themselves to build form. I love the spirit of the eucalyptus that holds the thought form of the tree with deep, focused concentration, refusing to be distracted by anything that might divert it from its task."

"With such concentration," Jesus reflected, "I wonder if the tree is aware birds build nests in its branches, that tiny bugs crawl up its trunk, and rain bathes its form."

Dora picked up another stem, "Or of soil covering its roots, or wind fluttering its leaves. Every kind of elemental interacts with each plant."

Maggie considered, "That one-pointed dedication is too much to ask. I can't imagine thinking of one thing all the time. They must get tired, or bored."

"They take vacations," Dora suggested. "During winter they leave their forms and play in the light with other elemental life. That's the reason leaves fall off trees. Their magnetic life force is not there to hold them on. In spring when they're through cavorting with their cohorts, they return to form and cause leaves to grow and blooms to bud again."

Maggie was excited at this new way of viewing the nature kingdom. "That's how they celebrate their return in the spring. We even call the seasons according to their activity. When the leaves fall, we call the season 'fall.' When leaves spring out, we call it 'spring.' It's interesting that we call leaves 'leaves' since they do leave."

They laughed in appreciation at her play on words and the truth behind it.

"That is the divine order of things," Jesus said. "Before we separated from God to experiment with form, we precipitated things when they were needed and let them etherealize when finished."

Maggie collected the roots and put them in a basket. "What if they were needed later?"

"Then they were summoned from etheric light substance to serve again. Between their times of usefulness, the elemental life was released to do other things." Jesus used the other basket to collect the leaves.

"That is the way things should be," Maggie commented. "It sounds like a beautiful existence. Then it would be impossible for anything to be where it isn't wanted. Like weeds."

Dora sighed dramatically, putting the back of her wrist on her forehead, "The scourge of my life."

They went inside to put the divided eucalyptus away.

"I have an idea," Jesus said, "May I weed your garden?"

"That would be lovely." Dora always accepted help immediately.

While Jesus was outside, Maggie helped Dora wash the eucalyptus roots and leaves. When Maggie looked out the window over the basin, Jesus stood, smiling, at the other end of the garden, his hands turned upward and arms spread.

"Dora! Look!" As they watched, he took a deep breath. Exhaling, he waved his left hand across the garden, moving his lips mysteriously. The weeds disappeared one by one as if swept away. Maggie dropped down on a stool in shock.

Dora stared and her mouth fell open. "Maggie, come back! Look at him."

Jesus laughed and rubbed his hands in gladness.

"I guess that all this talk about nature spirits manifesting and etherealizing made him want to try it. He's a very special boy. Shh. He's coming back in. He doesn't think we know."

Maggie busied herself away from the window, swirling leaves in water. Dora reached to get the gauze she used to hang drying herbs. When Jesus entered the room, they appeared to be absorbed in their tasks.

Maggie thought the silence rather awkward, but she couldn't think of anything to say. They should carry on a conversation now, or at least engage in friendly banter, but she couldn't take her mind off what she saw.

Dora saved the day, "Did you forget the hoe? The tools are in the shed by the garden."

He had a smug satisfied look, "I have everything I need."

Dora decided not to comment on his obvious lack of tools. "I understand. I like to do my weeding by hand too. Here. Have some water before you go back out." She sat a full mug on the table before him.

He had no words to reply. He was wary of telling them what he had done. His parents cautioned him not to use his talent for miracles for fear people would constantly pester him. They knew King Herod tried to have him killed at birth. They fled to Egypt and were on the run for a few years, but now, they tried to live a normal life in Nazareth.

He trusted Dora and Maggie and enthusiastically weeded the garden. In those moments, he naturally used the divine reality that he shared with all souls of earth. He forgot the unnatural practice of accepting limitation and working to get a job done. Now, he had no choice but to go out and waste time in the garden until the usual amount of time for weeding passed.

Dora watched from the window as he bent behind a stand of Echinacea. Was he going to mime the weeding now, just in case they looked out? "Perhaps it would have been kinder to act like it was normal to weed a garden in such a short time."

Maggie joined her at the window. "Maybe. Do you think we should tell him we saw him?"

"I don't know. I haven't experienced this before and handling this type of situation wasn't in the lessons on manners that my mother taught me."

They giggled together as they peered through the window. Maggie loved that Dora didn't have the pretentious superiority of many adults. As they watched, Jesus sat on the ground, legs folded. He appeared to be talking to a fern under a tree.

Maggie saw a ball of light in front of the fern. "Do you see that light?"

"Yes. I do." It took the form of a short and stubby little man with a round face, a stocking cap, and a long beard. They gasped in astonishment. "Oh my gosh!"

"Are you seeing what I'm seeing?" Maggie asked Dora.

"If you see a little man with a red hat and green shirt, the answer is 'yes.'"

"Okay. This is just too weird."

"Let's slice these apples and call him when he's finished visiting with that angel out there."

"Is that an angel?" Maggie asked. "I thought angels had wings."

Dora wasn't sure either. "Maybe it's a nature spirit like we were talking about on the porch."

"Whatever. We could ask Jesus."

Dora was cautious. "We can't do that. I don't think he wants us to know."

"He must be very sensitive. Maybe he knows we're watching him."

"I don't think everybody can see a gnome. Maybe he doesn't know we can see it."

"Well, the subject of nature spirits is bound to come up again," Maggie said. "You brought it up today. I'm going to ask him when I get a chance."

"I know you will. Let me know what you find out."

It wasn't long before Jesus came in again. They ate the apples and Dora asked Jesus some questions about his family and life in Nazareth. He had stories of his friend Jacob, the aggressive boy next door who intervened for him when others took advantage of his mild manner. He told of his group of seven friends who were serious about their studies and had philosophical discussions that far exceeded those of others their age and surpassed the expectations of the local chazzan.

Jesus and Maggie left Dora mystified. Didn't they make a pair! There could be no one like either of them. Surely they were destined to perform a profound service for God. Maggie had a curious mind and compassionate nature. Few young girls wanted to follow a healer on her rounds and Maggie saw the garden gnome, an unusual ability for anyone, young or old.

Dora wasn't surprised that she saw it herself. She saw unusual things when her guardian angel confirmed her conclusions about a patient's needs or gave her ideas for healing maladies. For several years she had felt the presence of the garden gnome, acknowledged and talked to it, but she hadn't seen it or heard it answer her prattling.

But she was sure that Jesus had. She wondered if the gnome had a message for her. What was its name? Should she care for the garden differently? What other spirits frequented her garden? What else should she plant? Should some herbs be used otherwise? She could learn much from nature spirits if she could only communicate with them!

What a unique young man Jesus was! Was he the long awaited messiah who would save Israel? And why were she and Maggie given the privilege of seeing his talents? Would they be involved in some way?

Dora's heart was full, but her mind kept yapping. Her exhilaration continued when she went to bed that night. Her mind wandered. What if Jesus were the messiah? What if he became king? What if he delivered the Israelites from their Roman oppressors? What if Maggie made a match with him and became queen?

Dora tossed and turned. Sleep eluded her. She dabbed clary sage under her nose, lay on her back, breathed consciously and rhythmically, and asked God's help to enter the silence. Peace put her calming hand on Dora's shoulders and entered her mind. She fell asleep at last and went deeper and deeper into the inner consciousness where all know all. She saw a young man, an older, mature Jesus sitting on a rock on a hill speaking effortlessly to a crowd in the valley below. The listening people were transfixed, enraptured by his message. Afterward, an older Maggie moved through the crowd followed by a cadre of women and girls. They sat on the bank of a calm sea listening to her every word. Jesus healed the sick. Maggie and Jesus were followed by a mass of humanity.

Dora came back to conscious awareness quickly, as if pulled by ropes. Her body felt heavy, her eyes fluttered open, and she recalled what she had seen. Her limbs draped sluggishly over the bed as she considered the ramifications of the revelation. Jesus and Maggie's life scripts put them together as teachers and healers. ~No wonder I was placed here in Magdala without family for no apparent reason. I am here to nurture and protect this special pair of souls.~ She doubted she could teach them. They were more likely to teach her. She reluctantly commanded her thoughts to discard the idea of them reigning over Israel. Their mission was not earthly, but spiritual. It appeared that the true concept of the messiah was directly opposite to that taught by the priests.

Dora rose to morning chores and made her rounds, still pondering the import of what she had learned. She knew that Jesus and Maggie had a short two and three years before their mitzvahs when they would become responsible adults. She wisely went about her usual business knowing that their life scripts would give them the right choices to spin them toward their destiny.

Maggie's thoughts wandered as she walked to the spring to fill the water vessels. She remembered meeting Jesus here at a similar time. Boys formed a stickball game near the well and she set her jars aside to join the game. The water could wait.

Just the thought of kicking Raamah's ass was enough to warrant being late with the water. Thanks to pitching lessons from Dan, she was the only one in Magdala who could do it. She guessed that Jesus could, but he didn't hold the same grudge against Raamah and his insultingly hilarious sidekick, Izaak. Besides, Jesus was in Nazareth.

Raamah was a trash talker. He ridiculed her for being a girl. That was interesting to Maggie. She supposed he did it because she had the audacity to play boys' games. He never presumed to inflict his sarcasm on Deborah or Lizette, but Lizette was the epitome of feminine grace. Maggie was as fascinated by Lizette as anyone. Her dark black hair was striking against her olive skin and dark brown eyes. She seemed unaware of her beauty, but her regal bearing inspired fascination and devotion in everyone, not just young boys. When Maggie went to the market with her, the vendors groveled for Lizette's attention, parading their wares ostentatiously.

Raamah was enamored of her. He was on his best behavior if he knew she was watching. Consequently, Lizette believed Raamah was an honorable boy of strong character and impeccable integrity. She didn't think he could be devious even when Maggie warned her of his disparaging manner.

And he looked good. He had dark hair with thick dark brows over deep set blue eyes. His complexion was tanned from the sun. His babyish cheeks made him look innocent and endeared him to gullible girls and indulgent women who wanted to pinch his cheeks, especially to Lizette who attracted him by unwittingly flashing her dimples at his amusing antics.

Lizette's guilelessness and innate goodness kept other women from being jealous of her. In fact, Maggie thought herself as attractive as Lizette; in a different way, of course. She didn't turn eyes, but she had more grace in her movement than Lizette who, though pretty, was gawky and uncoordinated. They were both adept at household arts, but Maggie's talent extended to music, gardening, animals, and sports. Maggie would certainly rather be herself than to be Lizette or anyone else.

Raamah was a good stickball pitcher. Maggie was sure he thought himself better than she. If his cohorts thought him inferior to Maggie in that regard, they certainly didn't share it with him. He was the leader of the pack and no one wanted to experience his displeasure, but they secretly applauded Maggie when she put him in his place.

Though he attracted girls and women, he made men and boys jealous. His eminence was not his own. It was reflected glory from his father, Eban, chief priest in the synagogue. Raamah was a privileged youth who would rise to a position of authority even if unmerited. He was haughty and treated the unfortunate with contempt. He was disdainful of Maggie because she thwarted his expectations for women. He knew it was her voice that floated over the rest from the court of women in the balcony. It angered him that a girl could effortlessly command such popular attention. He was infuriated that she presumed to excel at the masculine sport of stickball which should have been his bailiwick. She was on his turf and he wanted her out of the way.

She saw his look of disgust while he held the stick. Of course, he was the first up. No matter what he did, he assumed leadership, even though there were others of greater capability. That was fine with Maggie. She would put him out first thing.

Looking directly at the base, she lifted the ball before her eyes until she saw its two overlapping spheres point to the base, then stepped back, swung her arm backwards for momentum and threw the ball waist high over the base.

But Raamah didn't expect such accuracy and power. He swung low, expecting the pitch to be too weak to have height.

His teammates called encouragement behind him, "That's okay." "You'll get the next one."

He felt foolish. She made him look inept. He wished he had let Izaak go first so he could assess her ability without losing face. He adjusted his expectations for the next pitch. It would be placed properly if she was consistent.

She threw it with the same powerful accuracy. He swung too late, finding her pitch more powerful than he thought.

Now his reputation was on the line. Where did she learn to pitch like that? It was unnatural. Girls were reticent and sweet. They were weak, like flowers; pretty and resilient. But Mary Magdalene had always been more than other girls. She had a mind of her own.

He wiped the stick with his sleeve and got ready for the next pitch. He was wrong to expect her pitches to be weak or inaccurate. Both were strong and directly over the base. Now he knew how to hit it clear across the plaza.

Maggie watched him as he took his stance and moved back for more leverage. Aha! She drew him in. He expected her next pitch to be like the first two. Wouldn't he be surprised! She pitched slightly low and inside, just enough so he would think it true. If he did hit it, the ball would graze the ground.

He struck with a mighty swing, just in time for the ball to sail directly under his wrists. Frustrated, he threw the stick against the ground and swore. He looked at Maggie with murderous eyes. How dare she! But he was too vain and chauvinistic to believe she had outsmarted him with her wit and skill. He thought it was lucky or accidental. Girls couldn't pitch like that.

She had played with them before, when her brother, Dan, needed one more for his team. However, the first time it was her turn to pitch, the carpenter's son from Nazareth hit it way down the street, but Maggie had collided with Jesus, fallen, and left the game.

This was the second time she had pitched and it was his luck to be first up. He had never been so humiliated.

Disgusted, he walked away and sat on the low wall with his team.

Izaak was up next. He and Raamah fancied themselves best friends. They complemented each other. Where Raamah was brooding and dark, Izaak was lighthearted. He blindly followed Raamah. He always took Raamah's side. He thought this gave him popularity and prestige . . . and Maggie supposed it did – give him prestige anyway. They were popular, not because they were well-liked, but because they thought they were popular and exuded the aura of confidence and strength so strongly that everyone else assumed they were. Though people didn't like them, everyone wanted to be their friend.

Izaak swaggered to the plate and Maggie prepared. Izaak wanted to save face for Raamah. He decided to have some fun with her. He didn't care if he was hurtful. He just wanted everyone to think him funny and clever.

"Lucky pitch. Just throw it by me; I'll hit it to the sea. Forget that. I'll hit it all the way to Capernaum." He tapped the base with the stick. "Put it right there." He made a couple of ostentatious swings. Then he held the stick like an old man with a cane, insinuating that even an old man could hit one of her balls.

~He certainly is loose,~ thought Maggie as she aimed her next pitch. ~He's being foolish. If he thinks he can hit one of my pitches from that stance, he's wrong.~ She pitched it inside and weak. If he hit it, it wouldn't go far.

He didn't notice that it came straight at him until it was too late. He started to swing before realizing he should get out of the way. It rolled ineffectually off his left shoulder, a ball, not a strike.

"You yenta[1]! You hit me!" he roared, giving her a dirty look.

Maggie ignored his drama and picked up the rolling ball. She hadn't thrown it hard enough to hurt him that much. "I'll do better this time," she assured him. She lined up the ball in her usual way. He saw that the pitch was coming and scrambled to get ready. She threw it powerfully straight and true, but he expected it to be like the other one and was overly cautious. It flew by before he realized it was good.

---

[1] a vulgar shrew.

"Ball two!" he called.

Maggie knew it was good. "No. It was good. That's strike one."

A chorus of support came from her teammates. "Yeah, strike one."

"Ball two!" Izaak's team took his side, cupping their hands around their mouths to be even louder and more obnoxious. Pandemonium ensued, each team clambering for their side.

Maggie saw this wasn't going anywhere. This was a casual game. Its outcome didn't matter. She held up both hands for silence. A few players from both sides gestured for others to be quiet.

"Replay!" She bellowed in her most authoritative voice, the one she used when shouting instructions to her sheep dogs, Bo and Abbe.

Izaak's team sat back down and leaned forward in anticipation. Maggie set up to pitch.

She knew that Isaak meant to intimidate her into making it easy for him to look good, but she determined not to give in. Girls let boys have their way far too long. She knew women who always let men override their decisions, win at games, and use women's ideas as their own. She was out in the open now, pitching, a visible position of power. She would use it well. If she gave in, it would disappoint her team. More importantly, it would show both sides that women were weak, and men could continue to dominate.

She threw her best pitch again. Izaak's stick tipped it into the hands of Aaron, the catcher.

"Out!" Her team was quick to call the play.

Izaak wasn't going to show disappointment or anger, though he was furious. Enraged at Maggie for his failure to hit the ball and unwilling to blame himself, he attacked her. No, he didn't hit her. He wouldn't let anyone see him hit a woman. He used words.

"Maggie's a yenta who thinks she's a guy. Hissy, missy, she throws like a sissy."

Maggie fumed, but she didn't let anyone know she was insulted. Izaak called her a yenta and a sissy. How could she be both a vulgar shrew and a feminine boy? And Dan taught her well, she didn't throw like a girl!

She wanted to ask Izaak why he was unable to hit her pitches if they were so weak, but that would escalate things and she determined not to cave in. She remained calm. She would get one more player out and her team would be up.

Carmine was up next. Maggie liked Carmine. He could be a good guy when he wasn't around Raamah and Izaak, but he wanted them to like him and played along to impress them. In imitation of Izaak, he pranced to the plate. He had his own innocuous taunt. "If you dare, put it there." He positioned himself and raised the stick expectantly.

She gave him an honest pitch and he hit the ball far beyond the well. She wondered if it worried him that he had outdone Raamah in order to help the team.

Maggie helped field the ball.

Izaak was glib with his taunts. "Carmine got a hit. Maggie had a fit."

Yaar waited at first base for Tobias to throw to him from right field. But alas, Tobias fumbled the ball and Carmine raced to second where Enosh stood ready to make the catch that would tag him out. When Carmine rounded second, Maggie knew they had little chance of getting him out on third. "Throw it home!" By then Tobias recovered and sent the ball barreling toward the catcher, Aaron. Carmine ran back toward third and safety, but Aaron sent the ball sailing to Barak who tagged him out.

It was her team's turn to hit the ball, but Maggie knew that she couldn't stay. She had to get the water to the house. Unlike the boys, she was expected to help prepare supper and her mother needed the water. However, she was first up and decided to bat before she left. It wouldn't take very long.

She groaned when she saw Raamah as pitcher. Naturally. She knew this was coming.

She picked up the stick and stood ready for his revenge. She was tempted to strike out so that Raamah could keep his ego intact, but that wouldn't be true to herself. She resolved to do her best and finish making her statement.

The ball came violently. She ducked to avoid getting hit in the head. There was an intake of breath from all who saw, but it didn't shock Izaak who caught it and lobbed it back to Raamah.

"Ball one!"

Oh my! She'd better be ready for anything. She wanted this over as soon as possible. She would hit the next ball no matter how he pitched it. As soon as she saw him rev up, she shuffled her feet so she could shift forward or back to contact the ball. The ball was wide, but she hit it with a mighty swing. She didn't wait to see where it went.

Spectators cheered, "Go!" She started around the bases. Even if she didn't go far, she would be further away from Raamah and Izaak – even if they got her out. Approaching the first base, she saw outfielders fumble the ball. Her team urged her on.

"Run!" She didn't pause or waste time checking. They didn't expect her to run very fast because she was a girl.

"Keep going!" She went past second while Carmine struggled to retrieve a lousy throw from their outfielder.

"Go! Go! Go! Go!" Cheers swelled into a wild frenzy as she went around third while flustered opponents went crazy. She made home long before the ball rolled to Izaak. There was no doubt she had made it. Raamah and Izaak couldn't claim that she was out.

Raamah swore and threw his kippah[1] on the ground. Izaak paced behind the plate.

"Yenta!"

Her team gathered to congratulate her. Most were glad to see Raamah bested, especially by a girl. They all had suffered at his hands.

She gave her excuses and left the game to get the water. Dora sat on the edge of the well.

"You saw."

"Yes, that was a strong experience wasn't it?"

"I might have shaken things up a little bit."

"You know what you're doing?"

"Yes, I'm letting my light shine."

"I admire that about you. The priest's boy was mad."

"Yeah, if he'd been thinking, he would have thrown me a sissy pitch so I could only hit it a little way. But he doesn't think consciously. He lets anger get the best of him."

Once again, Dora was impressed that Maggie was such a keen observer of her own life. "Do you think he'll calm down?"

"Oh yes. Now that I'm out of the game, those boys will let him have his way."

"So you think you're the only one who opposes him."

---

[1] also known as a yarmulke. A hemispherical cap worn to fulfill the requirement that the head be covered at all times.

She nodded, "He's irrational. And there's something about me that makes him want to make my life miserable. Everyone else is afraid of him."

"You could avoid all this by being sweet and reticent like the other girls."

"Never."

CHAPTER 4

Maggie knew Jesus must return to Nazareth for school. He either came to Magdala for his one week off each month or stayed at his Uncle Jeremiah's farm south of Nazareth.

She loved being with him. He made everything more interesting and fun, but he wouldn't help her weave for the wedding! The sisters made everything Leora would wear. Sarina and Maggie would wear it when they got married. Leora wove the bridal gown on the large loom in the kitchen. Sarina made the headdress, and Maggie wove a broad sash. Leora had even more to do for she also wove a prayer shawl for Samuel to wear for the wedding.

Once the weaving was done, Leora's best friend, Batia, helped them decorate each piece with floral designs. Her embroidery was exquisite, fresh, and delicate. The stitches gleamed against the sheen of the fabric. She helped the others refine their designs. The day of the wedding, the girls would sprinkle their hair with scents from Dora's collection and weave flowers into their hair.

Samuel's family was equally busy. As sisters of the groom, Deborah and Janette made garments similar to Sarina and Maggie's. Nanette and Edita made the mothers' dresses. It was fun to sit in the shade and talk while doing the intricate needlework.

The more they did, the more there was to do. Each detail generated other ideas. The two households reached a creative peak. They tended their orchards and their vegetable and flower gardens. All summer, they gathered and dried fruit: figs, pomegranate, quince, star fruit, and apple. They stored almonds and collected eucalyptus honey.

The men experienced the same synergetic energy. Joseph was a skillful artisan. He designed the house and supervised workmen. When he returned to his family in Nazareth, he stayed busy, making chairs, a bed, a table, a chest. Leora and Samuel's serviceable furniture would be works of art. Jesus fashioned a special yoke for Samuel's oxen.

They did most of the work ahead of time. Like most girls, Leora had made linens and put them in a chest to await her marriage. There were beautiful napkins, towels, pillowcases, sheets, blankets, and a comforter. She had learned the art of pottery at her father's wheel and made a matched set of plates, bowls, jars, and serving dishes.

Leora was a diligent young lady who knew how to run a household. Samuel was an industrious young man with a viable trade. He was a clever fisherman who traded in the market. Fish would be served at the wedding feast.

Both families had Essene discipline, rising before sunrise to commune with the forces of nature, ritual bathing in cold water; laboring in the fields and orchards until the heat of the day, eating meals of fruit, vegetables, and grains. They observed periods of silence and devoted evenings to study and communion with heavenly light.

Enoch and Jonathan's families did not adhere to the Essene custom of wearing white linen, for that would make their spiritual persuasion too obvious to those who lived according to the corrupted Mosaic Law that prevailed in the land. Their children associated freely with other children in the community, went to synagogue, and participated in local festivals.

Leora and Samuel were well matched, but their siblings were likely to marry local youth outside the fellowship as they were isolated from the Brotherhood. They hoped to find spouses who were, at least, tolerant of their way of living.

The Sabbath was given to study, discussion, visiting, singing, and playing. Families dressed their best for synagogue. Today, Samuel would recite ancient blessings from the Torah because it was the Sabbath before his marriage to Leora.

The women went to their area apart from the men. The girls carried pouches full of nuts and dried fruit to toss above Samuel's head after his reading.

They laughed mischievously as they sat on the long bench beside Edita and Nanette. Maggie had gone to weddings as a child, but this was her first time to participate. While helping with the preparations, she had plied Edita and Leora with numerous questions.

Maggie heard other snickers and looked around to see Lizette come in with her mother. She and Deborah scooted together to make room for her. They showed each other the contents of their pouches. Lizette's was as full as theirs. Most of the other girls carried pouches too.

The congregation settled into quiet expectation, but the girls could hardly sit still. They whispered and giggled, squirmed and turned. Maggie was hyperaware of everything. Sarina motioned to Maggie, Deborah, and Lizette to be quiet. Maggie couldn't understand how Sarina and Janette were able to remain so calm and poised, serene and peaceful. She supposed they thought themselves too mature to show excitement. Maggie scoffed at such restraint. She hoped that she never became so staid that she didn't freely enjoy these special celebrations.

The priest, Eban, droned on and on, reciting prayers incessantly. Finally, he announced Samuel and Maggie sat upright to listen carefully. Leora left her seat and moved close to the dais. Samuel spoke boldly, with assurance, intoning the reading from the Torah in his smooth baritone. Everyone seemed to listen more attentively today. She assumed it was the novelty of having a different reader who put new meaning into the ancient words. When Samuel finished, Leora stood beside him. Young girls showered them with nuts and dried fruit from their pouches, wishing them a sweet and fertile life together.

Later, Maggie asked Leora why she joined Samuel after his reading. "I don't remember other brides doing that." ~Wasn't it bold to display herself that way?~

"I'm an eager bride, Maggie. I love Samuel and want to share everything. He asked me to come forward so we could be together for the blessing of God and good wishes of the people. People may talk, but they'll find other things to talk about soon. I don't want my wedding to be like everyone else's. I want it to be memorable. I want it to be right for Samuel and me. It might not be right for everyone else, but it'll be right for us."

Maggie admired Leora's resolve and hoped she would have the same integrity when her turn came.

The evening before the wedding, Edita mixed dough for the challah bread[1], kneaded, let it rise, and punched it down. She shaped it into long rolls, braided them, put them in pans, sprinkled them with sesame seeds, and left them to rise overnight. She rose early to bake them.

They planned for Leora to sleep late on her wedding day. No one called her to help with breakfast. It was her last day to live in her childhood home and she wouldn't be here for breakfast any more. Maggie thought it just as well. Maggie would still go out to milk Elsie, gather the eggs from the chickens, then set the table and pour the milk. Sarina would take Leora's place in the kitchen.

When Maggie came in from the barnyard, she was surprised to see Leora's friend, Batia, already there and Leora slicing bread and fruit as usual. "I thought you would relax in bed until time to go to the Mikveh[1] for your purification."

"I was too excited to stay in bed. You are all so sweet to make this day for me. I appreciate it so much. I love the scarf you made for my veil, Sarina, and the sash you made, Maggie, and the beautiful embroidery, Batia. Papa and Dan, thank you for building the house with Joseph, Jesus, Jonathan, and Samuel and for moving my things. Mama, thank you for growing the food with Nanette and preparing for the feast.

"Most of all, I love the way you raised me. Unlike other girls I learned to read. I learned the domestic arts, not like my wealthy friends who have servants do everything. I'm grateful that I know how to work.

"Thank you for having me, for being my mother, father, sisters, brother, and friend." Happy tears welled in their eyes. Edita wiped hers away with her sleeve. Dan rounded the table to engulf Leora in a brotherly hug, Batia embraced her from the side, Maggie grabbed her around the waist, and Sarina slipped under her arm on the other side. Enoch and Edita held each other's arms around their children.

Edita was overcome with joy and sadness. "I love you, Leora. Thank you for being my daughter."

Even Enoch's eyes watered. He squeezed Leora's shoulder. "I'm very happy for you. I know you're in good hands with Samuel."

Dan was less affected, "It won't be that different." He relaxed his hold. "You'll still be in Magdala." Making light of the situation he

---

[1] a Jewish braided bread eaten at celebrations.
[1] a bath for ritual immersion. 'Mikveh' means a 'collection' – a collection of water.

turned to the others. "We'll see Leora all the time. Samuel will still be my best friend. We'll keep doing things together. Our families will be one family now."

Leora was fasting until after her spiritual purification in the Mikveh, but she drank a draught of water while the others ate breakfast amid excited chatter. Everything was ready for the wedding and the feast afterward. Edita's culinary talents were legendary and the women of Magdala helped with the preparations under her guidance. Last minute details were delegated to friends and their servants. Edita had little else to do on the day of the wedding. The two families would spend the day together.

Enoch secured the wedding apparel inside a trunk, hitched the horse to a cart, and took their things to the synagogue. They rode the short distance to the synagogue where Nanette, Janette, and Deborah waited in the bride's room. The women donned ritual white linen and entered the Mikveh for Leora's purification ritual. Edita and Nanette kissed Leora on both cheeks and her friend, sisters, and new sisters-in-law greeted her with more hugs and kisses. Leora faced the steps of the Mikveh with the mothers and they descended into the waste-deep pool. They cradled her gently as she leaned back to immerse her head in the water. This consciously washed away the old to make room for the new life with Samuel to flow in. The girls joined them in the pool and they sang songs of joy, love, wisdom, fertility, prosperity, and exemplary family life.

Thoroughly cleansed, they slipped into dry robes and entered the next room where Edita and Nanette served dark, sweet wine. They rubbed Leora's body with perfumed oils, keeping her warm with heated towels. It was her day and they served her in every way. The girls sang, passed fruit, and served Leora, not allowing her to feed herself. The whimsical innocence intrigued Maggie. She hoped to be nurtured in the same way when her turn came.

Dora arrived with a case of flowers, herbs, and oils for them to choose scents and decorate their hair. Sarina and Janette perfumed Leora's hair and combed it into a cascade of flowing black tresses strung with flowers. Edita draped the wedding dress on Leora's shoulders. Maggie tied the sash that she had made in a flattering bow in the back.

Leora sat on a throne-like chair and Deborah opened the door to the female guests. Women and girls brought gifts and wished her well. Lizette came early. Maggie felt sorry for her friend who had neither siblings of her own nor the closeness of sisters. Maggie and Deborah decided to share the rest of the day with Lizette. Family time was over. Now was the time for friends. The family made the rounds to ensure that every guest felt welcome.

Clusters of women exclaimed over gifts and compared the wedding party with those of the past. Maggie, Lizette, and Deborah stopped talking when they felt the room grow silent. Everyone's eyes were on the latest guest. The priest's wife, Zadika, entered with her handmaiden. Her presence commanded attention. Zadika awed everyone because she was the priest's wife. She invariably occupied the front row of the women's loft, consistently sat straight in her pew with Hannah beside her, paid close attention to the service, and closed her eyes and held her hands in a prayerful position at the right times. She was the epitome of propriety and greeted all the congregants with quiet decorum. She cared about people, but was never overt. She was not demonstrative and seldom put herself forward in social situations. When others tried to be friendly, she responded with direct answers that left no room for discussion. She seemed to hide something.

Lizette gushed over Zadika's clothes. She dressed simply and wore the best fabrics styled with understated elegance. Her walk was graceful and smooth. Women admired but were not jealous of her quiet, fragile beauty. If not for her status as priest's wife, she would disappear into the woodwork.

The women watched respectfully as she approached Leora with her gift. "This is for the center of your home to remind you and Samuel of the presence of God among you."

Leora opened a beautiful hand woven altar cloth. She admired its beauty and exclaimed over the fine workmanship. Sarina and Janette folded it carefully and placed it with the other presents.

Edita graciously thanked Zadika for her thoughtful generosity, raised her wine glass, and faced the other women who lifted theirs. "We are gathered to help Leora start her married life.

"Leora, you are very fortunate to marry a man from a family that is close friends with your own. You know what to expect from your union. You and Samuel know to forget yourself in favor of what is best for the both of you. You know the womanly arts, he knows the manly ones. You know how to help him with his manly challenges.

He knows how to help you with the womanly ones. He will go out and secure a living. You will keep the home for him and make it a sanctuary of love, beauty, and comfort.

"You are fortunate that you already love Samuel. Never take that love for granted. Nurture it every day. Find things to appreciate about him and show him your gratitude. Try to do more for him than he does for you. In marriage and life, you get what you give. Your life is a reflection of what you give. If you give encouragement, you are encouraged. If you give love, it springs back to you."

Edita drank from her glass and stepped back and Nanette stepped forward to lift hers. "I'm happy that you are marrying my son and that you love him. He has grown to be a fine man.

"Let him know what you want. When you are sure it is reasonable, demand it of him. He is gentle and loving. He will do his best to please you, but never demand anything you know he cannot give.

"Because he will go out of the home to make his way, he will have trials and cares that you don't see. Your only way of knowing what he encounters is for him to tell you. Encourage him to talk about his day and listen carefully. Never judge, for that interrupts the flow of communication. Encourage him in the right and hold the immaculate thought in all situations and conditions. Expect the best and you will get it.

"If you are tempted to get discouraged, disown unwanted earthly conditions and claim what you want from God. Say, 'Hate and fear be gone. I claim love, peace, and joy.' Be vigilant in your applications, affirmations, and invocations; live to experience them and make them so in every thought, feeling, word, and deed."

She led the women in their next drink.

Batia stepped forward. "I call twelve young girls with the gifts of God."

The children wore circlets of flowers representing spiritual qualities. The girls were cute, innocent with the freshness of childhood, and solemnly participated in the ceremony.

The first wore a circlet of fern and gave Leora a single stem. "I give you this fern for protection of your home and family."

The second wore a crown of Queen Anne's lace. "I give you Queen Anne's lace for wisdom.

The third, "I give a pink rose for love and devotion."

The fourth, "I give a white lily for purity and a daisy for hope."

The fifth, "I give nasturtium for healing."

Sixth, "I give honeysuckle for grace."

Seventh, "I give crepe myrtle for exemplary family life and violets for forgiveness."

Eighth, "I give lilacs for remembrance."

Ninth, "I give alyssum for harmony and balance."

Tenth, "I give mustard for abundance and clover for peace."

Eleventh, "I give daffodils for joy."

Twelfth, "I give an iris for the feminine principle."

Leora took each of the flowers graciously. When they were clustered in her arms, she thanked the maidens. "I accept these gifts for the blessing of my home." Batia tied a pretty white ribbon around them to make a lovely bouquet for Leora to carry down the aisle.

The women joined their families in the shade of the olive trees in the synagogue's courtyard. The guests sang joyously when Leora appeared at the gate. Sarina stood by her holding the ornate veil she had made and Janette held Samuel's prayer shawl. Samuel greeted her in his kitel[1] and white cap. He lovingly veiled her face and Leora spread the tallit across his shoulders to symbolize the protection she gave him with her love. Wearing the prayer shawl, he met Enoch at a table in the corner to sign the ketubah[2] that documented his obligations to Leora, enumerated his bride price for her, and listed the content of her dowry bestowed by Enoch. He pledged to 'work for her, honor, provide for, and support her, in accordance with the practices of Jewish husbands.'

Jonathan and Nanette escorted their son, Samuel, to the dais and he stood under the open sky with Dan, his best friend and almost brother-in-law. Eban chanted the priestly blessing of welcome as Enoch and Edita escorted Leora to Samuel. Batia and the couple's sisters followed and waited while Leora circled him seven times to build the boundaries of sacred space for their union and took her place on his right. The families fell in line on each side.

Samuel said, "Be sanctified to me as my wife according to the tradition of Moses and Israel," and they promised each other, "We shall build our lives together through equality and cooperation, understanding and admiration, mutual respect and honesty. We

[1] white robe worn on special occasions.
[2] Jewish prenuptial agreement.

pledge to support and trust each other through life's challenges, to share together moments of joy and of sorrow, to be sensitive to each other's needs, and encourage each other to lead lives of fulfillment. Through our love and values we will create a home committed to Torah and our Jewish heritage, a home filled with love and friendship, peace and harmony, benevolence and charity."

Eban closed, "This covenant of marriage is signed and sealed according to the laws and traditions of Moses and the people of Israel."

Samuel spoke the Kiddushin[1], "You are consecrated to me with this ring in accordance with the religion of Moses and Israel." He placed a ring on her finger to represent the wholeness achieved through marriage and a hope for an unbroken union.

Eban gave thanks to God for the opportunity to perform this mitzvah and read the marriage contract for all to hear.

Dan, Jonathan, and Enoch took turns reading the seven blessings over a cup of wine.

1. Praised are You, O Lord our God, King of the Universe, Creator of the fruit of the vine.

2. Praised are You, O Lord our God, King of the Universe, Who created all things for Your glory.

3. Praised are You, O Lord our God, King of the Universe, Creator of man.

4. Praised are You, O Lord our God, King of the Universe, Who created man and woman in Your image, fashioning woman from man as his mate, that together they might perpetuate life. Praised are You, O Lord, Creator of man.

5. May Zion rejoice as her children are restored to her in joy. Praised are You, O Lord, Who causes Zion to rejoice at her children's return.

6. Grant perfect joy to these loving companions, as You did to the first man and woman in the Garden of Eden. Praised are You, O Lord, who grants the joy of bride and groom.

7. Praised are You, O Lord our God, King of the Universe, who created joy and gladness, bride and groom, mirth, song, delight and rejoicing, love and harmony, peace and

---

[1] sanctification or dedication, the first of the two stages of the Jewish wedding process.

companionship. O Lord our God, may there ever be heard in the cities of Judah and in the streets of Jerusalem voices of joy and gladness, voices of bride and groom, the jubilant voices of those joined in marriage under the bridal canopy, the voices of young people feasting and singing. Praised are You, O Lord, Who causes the groom to rejoice with his bride.

Samuel and Leora drank from the wine glass. Dan, as best man, wrapped the glass in a cloth and placed it on the ground. Samuel stomped it with his right foot to show that their marriage was as permanent as the shatters of the glass.

The guests sang and followed the couple to the other side of the square where tables waited for the feast. The guests proceeded to entertain the newlyweds.

Guests circled by Samuel and Leora to congratulate them saying "Mazel tov," acknowledging that a great blessing occurred.

The events of Leora's wedding repeated in Maggie's mind for the next several days. When she stirred Dora's pot, she thought of God's creating plants to show His glory. She knew he created Dora's plants to heal people.

"The fourth wedding blessing said that God created man and woman in his image that they might have children together. Does the fifth blessing mean that man and woman are restored to the human family through marriage?"

Dora sliced through a handful of leaves to release their healing potential. "In the Jewish tradition, marriage perpetuates our kind. Single men are not allowed to be rabbis. Unmarried men who seek fulfillment outside the home don't set a good example for congregants. Marriage returns them to the fold where they find satisfaction with a good wife. That deepens spiritual awareness and commitment."

"Do men and women have to get married to find joy?"

"In a good marriage, they find joy in one another because they please and support each other, share everything, and are sensitive to each other's needs. They've pledged to create a home with the feeling nature of the Mother God." Dora slipped the leaves into the stock Maggie stirred.

"You can have that without being married. I have it at home with Mama and Papa."

"You're blessed with a solid home, Maggie. Enoch and Edita set a good example for Leora as Jonathan and Nanette do for Samuel. They'll do well with their own home. It's natural for children to create a life of their own.

"You can see that God loves to create and his creations love to co-create with him. Plants multiply and large trees grow from tiny seeds. Sheep birth lambs, usually two at a time. Man and woman are made in God's image. Being like him, they have the creative impulse and love to procreate."

Maggie lifted her spoon, let its contents spill, and checked its color and tint. "That's sex. Right?"

"Yes."

"So why are we taught that sex is a dirty, nasty sin?"

"Unfortunately, parents teach youth to avoid sex because it makes babies. Parents manipulate them to think it's bad and convince them to wait until they are married and can make a good home for children. That's the reason children are taught to hide their bodies. It's why girls are chaperoned when in the company of boys."

Indignant, Maggie put her hand on her hip. "But now, after holding back for so long, it's okay for Leora and Samuel to have sex."

"Yes, it's encouraged."

Maggie stopped stirring, shocked at the thought.

"Remember, you and the other girls showered nuts over them wishing them fertility. The crowd applauded after the blessings," Dora explained. "The bride and groom left the wedding feast early to go to the nuptial bed. Everyone expects them to have sex, especially their mothers and fathers, because they want grandchildren to love."

This was all too much for Maggie. "How can we be expected to stop being ashamed of our bodies and suddenly allow ourselves to have sex after so much sinful training."

Dora laughed, "It doesn't make sense does it? Fortunately, desires set in and sex comes naturally."

This gave Maggie a lot to think about.

Maggie entered Dora's hut with concern on her face. A messenger stood outside in the dusk meaning someone was critically ill or in labor. Dora answered the question she saw on Maggie's face while she packed some choice jars of tea, oils, and balms.

"It's Zadika. She's having asphyxiating attacks. She's unable to breathe. I must get over there before the life force leaves her body."

"Zadika? Eban's wife! And they sent for you?" Maggie grabbed the water vessel and Dora's medicine bag.

"Yes, it must be really bad."

They took to the road following Zadika's handmaiden. "Maggie, this is Hannah. She'll work with us."

Some people in Magdala avoided using Dora's skills at all costs. Priests considered her methods questionable, bordering on sorcery, but they tolerated her practice because many adored her for helping them. It was unheard of for a priest's household to invite her to attend the lady of the house. However, Zadika had contacted Dora before. Wearing plain robes with her face covered, she stealthily entered Dora's hut to purchase a breathing concoction. Dora thought that her present condition was related to difficulty in breathing and prepared accordingly.

Zadika used the power of her position to assist the hungry poor of Magdala. She and Hannah secretly came to Dora for remedies to common ailments and shared them with suffering peasants. Dora knew that Zadika hid this from her husband.

Though Zadika was a compassionate servant of God, she led a tortured life, being told what to do and not do by Eban. As a priest's wife, Jewish law bound her to the approved practices of priests. When those methods didn't work or were unjust, she ignored the guilt in her gut and found better ways. She was torn between what she was allowed to do and the promptings of her heart. Dora suspected that Zadika's guilty feelings caused her breathing problems. ~What a burden to be married to such a man! And that son of hers!~

Dora left her opinions at the door as she entered Eban's palatial home and followed Hannah to Zadika's quarters. Zadika strained against the bed in futile attempts to take in air. Her eyes bugged wildly and her throat wheezed as her glottis blocked her efforts. It seemed determined to choke the life out of her body.

Dora stroked the woman's forehead with a cool cloth, "Did you swallow something?"

She tried to answer, but could not wrench a word out of her constricted throat.

"Don't try to talk. Just shake your head yes or no."

Zadika shook her head.

"Your son will help us move you."

Dora beckoned to the son, "Help us take her outside. She needs fresh air."

Maggie took the foot of Zadika's pallet. The son quickly grabbed the end at her head. They laid her on a long bench on the balcony. Maggie's focus was on Zadika and her needs, but her awareness reached out to recognize the son. ~Raamah! ~

This was Raamah's mother. In the stress of the moment, he didn't put on airs and forgot to intimidate anyone. In his concern for his mother, he was helpful and accommodating. His usual personality disappeared. Fear made him vulnerable and accessible with a caring and humble attitude. She had not dreamed he had that in him.

Zadika's chest heaved in vain attempts to squeeze air through her inflamed throat.

Dora pulled Maggie aside, "The only thing I can do is cut her throat to give her some air but, bleeding would weaken her. Go get Jesus while I try to postpone the inevitable."

Aghast, Maggie's head tilted back when she understood the implications of Dora's order. Without asking questions, she ran to Jonathan and Nanette's where Jesus stayed. Not having time for pleasantries, she went directly to the roof where he slept. "Jesus!" She called into the open space on the rooftop. Bodies asleep on the floor stirred in response to her racket. "Jesus!" He sat up quickly. Seeing which pallet was his, she quickly went to him. "Jesus, Dora needs your help."

He responded to her frantic voice, slipped on his sandals, and followed her down the stairs, through the street, and into the palace. Raamah was still there and Maggie wished to allay his suspicions. "Jesus has the poultice."

Dora was relieved to see him. Jesus looked at her reluctantly.

"Raamah, go to the cistern for more water, Dora ordered. I need to bathe your mother." Raamah hurried from the room.

She gestured toward the couch and told Jesus the situation. "She can't breathe. I can't do anything for her. Her throat is constricted so I can't give her tea or scented oil. She cannot inhale or swallow."

She read his reservations, "Jesus, you can trust Maggie and me."

He approached the pallet and the woman who no longer tried to breathe, whose heart barely pulsated.

"Let's move her into her chambers." They quickly moved the pallet to the bed inside. Maggie and Dora hurriedly drew the curtains.

"Spread a stinky poultice on her chest." Maggie found the most pungent of the lot and did as he said. She smoothed a menthol balm liberally, thinking that the stench alone would make anyone think it's a panacea for all ills.

Jesus said, "Zadika, you are free to live a full life. Open yourself to creativity and joy."

Her eyes fluttered, her pulse grew stronger, her throat opened, and mucus slid down her stomach to pass through her body.

Maggie opened windows on each side of the room as Dora spread Zadika's arms to open her chest to the fresh night air. Jesus found warm broth on the sideboard. He lifted her to a sitting position and put it to her lips. She sipped it gratefully.

Raamah entered the room thinking he was delivering the water that would bathe his mother for burial. Instead, she sat, eating hungrily with light in her eyes. Fortunately, the water vessel was leather. Otherwise it would have broken when he dropped it on the floor.

Jesus moved aside to make room for the son. Raamah embraced his mother, shamelessly crying tears of joy. Maggie and Dora observed the touching scene and adjusted their opinion of Raamah. ~Maybe he's not so bad after all,~ Maggie thought.

Dora minimized Jesus's role in Zadika's healing, "Thank you for coming with Maggie to deliver the poultice. We needed two strong men to get the water and move the pallet. You can go now." She gestured to Hannah, who rushed in at the sound of the fallen water vessel. "Let's wash the sickness out of the room."

Zadika clasped Dora's hand, "I don't know how to thank you."

Dora squeezed hers in return, "No need, Lady Zadika. You are vital to the well-being of Magdala. We are all grateful for your service to the poor. I'm only thankful we could help you continue that."

Hannah was bathing Zadika and cleaning the room when they left.

Maggie had many questions when she walked home with Dora in the early morning. "What did you mean when you said Zadika serves the poor?"

"She's a righteous, just, and pious woman well suited to life as priest's wife. She organizes women to feed the poor and help them do things they couldn't do alone. Though she could be a selfish, idle woman, she selflessly goes out to help people. If she finds someone in need of healing while delivering food, she sends Hannah for my help. I give her the medicine and tell her what to do. Hannah's becoming a proficient healer."

"Does Eban know?

"No, she does it at great risk. She hides it from him for fear he would put a stop to it."

"You sent Raamah away. I take it he doesn't know."

"He's a devoted son, but he, like his father, is blind to her strength and eminence as a caring, compassionate woman. I don't think what he saw tonight registered to him. He probably knows little more than he did."

"I noticed his expression of distaste when he saw us."

"He knows his father's disdain for natural healing. As a loyal son, Raamah believes his father can do no wrong. He's training to follow in his father's footsteps."

"It must be a great strain for her to maintain that façade."

"Yes, and she absorbs her husband's contempt and turns it in on herself. Hence, her energy doesn't flow freely and blocks her breathing."

"So that's the reason Jesus told her 'You are free to live a full life. Open yourself to creativity and joy.' How did he know?"

"We know he's gifted. She has enormous compassion for others. It would be great if she accepts compassion for herself. I hope she will live fully with a clear conscience."

CHAPTER 5

Every year, Jewish men anticipated going to Jerusalem for Passover. Maggie was almost eleven, not yet of age. Her sister, Sarina, came of age in the fall and Maggie would be bat mitzvah in the late summer more than a year later. Maggie would progress with Deborah and Lizette though she was a few months younger than they.

When Maggie learned that boys who were of age were qualified to go to Jerusalem to celebrate Passover, she assumed that girls were too. When Edita gently told her that it didn't apply to girls and women were not required to go, Maggie was even more determined for Sarina to go and the whole family with her. Sarina was reluctant to put herself forward. She would not insist on going herself. She was reticent to disturb the status quo, but wouldn't oppose Maggie when she insisted on having things her way. Neither would she encourage Maggie or be an accomplice to the machinations that she devised with overarching enthusiasm. The path of least resistance was Sarina's way.

Maggie took stock of the situation. She was sure that Enoch and Edita would take their family if Jonathan and Nanette took theirs. She knew that the men usually saw Essenes who had lived with them at Mount Carmel so many years ago. Edita and Nanette hadn't seen the women they knew there since moving to Magdala and starting their families. That was twenty years ago. Maggie would find a way to influence them.

The next time she washed clothes with Sarina and their mother, she got her to talk about the old days at Mount Carmel. "Mother, what was it like in the Essene community?"

Edita swished the clothes through the soapy water, her eyes turning reflective. "It was heaven. I liked living with so many people who think as I do. We did everything together and shared everything equally.

"We lived expecting God to abundantly supply our needs without struggle from us. We studied ancient writings in Hebrew, Sanskrit, and Greek and learned about health, agriculture, and astronomy. Nature was our best teacher. It was a simple life. We rose early to watch the sunrise and reflect on the beauty of nature, commune with nature spirits, and give thanks to them. We bathed in cold water and put on white linen garments, then spent the day working in the fields while singing."

"What songs did you sing?"

"Songs in praise of the elements of sun, water, wind, and earth; life and joy, power, love, wisdom, war, peace, trees, stars, moon, Mother Earth, and Father. Songs of lament and prophecy. You've learned some in the fields."

"I know the ones to sun, air, water, and earth."

Maggie wrung soapy water out of a indigo tunic. "Did you sing them with Nanette and Jesus' mother, and her cousin, Elizabeth?"

"Yes, and between growing seasons we sang while we wove."

"Did you gossip and laugh like we do when we get together?"

"Not much gossip. We lived our lives consciously, improvising them as we were inspired. We didn't overreact to people's mistakes or blow them out of proportion like gossips do. And we were isolated from political upheaval, detached from finite things. It was an idyllic existence. We didn't use our thoughts, feelings, and words to reflect negative makings. Instead, we extended the light of the Heavenly Father and divine feeling of the Earth Mother."

She handed another tunic to Maggie to wring for the rinse.

"We ate in silence in order to breathe long and deeply to absorb the blessing of the angel of air. We chewed our food into liquid so it could be blessed by the angel of water who turned it into blood. We ate slowly and mindfully in praise to the Lord so his power could enter us. We ate only when we were hungry but never ate until we were full and we fasted one day a week. We ate fruits and vegetables in season. We never ate cooked food."

Maggie lowered a tunic into the rinse. "You mean you ate your meat raw?"

"No. We never ate meat or anything that had to be burned to make it palatable."

"I've heard you say 'Earth Mother' twice today. You don't use that term very often."

"We live among traditional Jews. The priests discourage Jews from acknowledging the Mother God. In their view, God is a patriarch, masculine, without feminine qualities, and each life stream can only have one of those types of energies. They don't understand that masculine and feminine qualities should be balanced in everyone. They think that such an idea is an abomination that negates the concept of the One God. They don't understand that God is over, under, around, and interpenetrates us and every existing thing. We are all points of light in the one mind of God. All in one. One in all. Men are not more whole than women. Women are not more whole than men. Each person is a unique balance of masculine and feminine. Unfortunately, even the Essenes exalt men over women. They hold all the leadership roles, except for Judy, who is a prophetess who channeled messages from the ensouling spirit of our activity."

"Does that mean women did all the work?"

"Oh no, everyone was always busy. Even men were required to live there a while before they could be part of the leadership."

"Were there leaders among the women?"

"Not formally. Capable women helped others. We worked together synergetically to get things done. Big decisions rarely had to be made. The real one was already made – to live together in sisterhood and love. We were together through consensus rather than vote. It was a holistic and flexible way of doing things. We loved to support and cooperate with one another. In truth we had our own organization, but it was holistic, not hierarchical like the men's.

"We spent a third of the nights of each year studying the Law and worshipping together."

"Why haven't you told us all this before? You've kept it from us a long time." Maggie continued outrageously. "Look at us! We're grown!"

The others roared with laughter. Edita started to answer the question, but Sarina's contagious laughter welled up again. For some reason she could not stop laughing. Maggie couldn't keep from laughing either, though she hadn't thought there was anything that funny. "Why are you laughing?"

Sarina almost couldn't get the words out from laughing so hard, but she managed a blurted imitation of Maggie. "Look at us! We're grown!"

Maggie still didn't think that so funny, but she couldn't keep from giggling because Sarina's waves of uncontrolled laughter were so overwhelming they filled the whole room. When it subsided, Maggie wiped tears from her eyes, still convulsing.

"Really Mother, why haven't you told us about your time with the Essenes before?"

"I thought you were too young to be discreet. If I sang the songs about Mother God and praises to the sun, the moon, and the elements, you would learn them and sing them at your chores. A traditional Jew might hear as they passed and accuse us of not believing in the One God. Few people understand that we are all God's children, with light bodies that make us a part of God."

"And you didn't eat meat. Didn't you make animal sacrifices to wipe out your sins at Passover?"

"No, we offered ourselves for the light of God to shine through us to save the world."

"Those were wonderful friends."

"Yes, we were very close. But we're scattered now. I never see Mary who's living in Nazareth, though I do see Joseph and Jesus. When they come here to build, she stays in Nazareth to care for her large family. Miriam lives in Cana, and Elizabeth in Hebron. Enoch brings news of her when he and Dan, Jonathan and Samuel go to Jerusalem.

"Josada is in Bethany. They stay with her and Simon and their three children, Lazarus, Martha, and Young Mary when they go to Passover and use Joseph of Arimathea's home in the Essene district of Jerusalem as a meeting place. He has a large compound. I don't know where Sophie is. Jose is with Mary and Joseph. She cared for Jesus when they were in Egypt.

Maggie could see Edita felt nostalgic about her old friends. "Mama, let's go to Jerusalem and see all your friends."

"What a wonderful reunion that would be!" Edita said wistfully.

Maggie didn't give her time to think again. She threw her arms around Edita and kissed her. "It sure would, Mother. I'm going to go tell Nanette and Leora."

Maggie skipped to Leora's where she and her friend Batia made bread with Nanette and Janette. Maggie thought that Janette's being there was propitious, as she was bat mitzvah this year with Sarina.

She would be here to listen while Nanette reminisced about old friends and bygone days.

Leora was glad to see Maggie. "Come in and help us with the bread."

Maggie worked and visited with the others. "Nanette, are we making the bread like you and Mother did when you were in Heaven at Mount Carmel?"

"How did you know about that? Has Edita been talking?"

"Just this morning. She thinks we're old enough to know."

Batia looked up from the flour that she was measuring. She had heard of the strange spiritual preferences of Leora's parents, but never heard them first hand.

"Hmm," Nanette worked the dough with her fingers and palms. "The elemental spirits prepared our bread. The earth spirit nurtured the wheat. We gathered it, then invoked the water spirit by adding water then we left it outside so the air spirit could embrace it and the fire spirit expanded it. The wheat sprouted with the blessing of the elements. Then we crushed the sprouted grain and made wafers to put out in the sun. They rose in praise to the Earth Mother. At the middle of the day, we turned it over so the fire spirit could brown the other side."

Batia was fascinated by these curious customs. "I never knew that the sun was hot enough to bake bread."

"It does quite well actually. It takes longer and the bread doesn't get as crusty on the outside, but it is more flavorful and digests easier. Very healthy."

Maggie had the right question to ask that would make Nanette want to go to Jerusalem. "I didn't ask Mother why it was called Heaven at Mount Carmel. Can you tell us?"

"It was a tranquil place, away from the world. Freedom from conflicting dogma. Free to express ourselves in our own way and talk and sing without censure. Free from restrictions on women. Surrounded by the tranquility of nature: the trees, sea, breeze, and sun. Perfect peace."

The girls' hands slowed as they kneaded the bread to activate the yeasties. Nanette was lost in thought. "I loved those heavenly qualities, but being with my friends was like living with angels. There was Mary, the angel of healing, Edita, the angel of cooking, Miriam, the angel of faith, Diana, the angel of compassion, and Sophi, the angel of wisdom.

"What angel are you, Nanette?"

"Nanette smiled at the whimsical turn of the conversation. "I guess I'm the gardening angel."

Maggie had her where she wanted her. "Wouldn't it be great if you could see them all again?"

Nanette laughed.

"You could meet their children, talk about old times, and learn what they're doing now."

"Whoa, where could I do this?"

"In Jerusalem."

"When?"

"At Passover."

"Women don't go to Passover." That concluded the matter for Nanette. She didn't take it seriously.

"But they can. Mother would like to go."

"She and I see each other anyway. The other women would have to come to make it worthwhile."

"They could come easily. Their men always go. Papa and Dan talk about them when they come back."

"How do we get them to come?"

"There must be a way."

Leora loved the idea. "Nanette, you and Mother could write a letter to all the women you know. We could make copies. If all of them invited their friends where they live, there would be a lot of women and we could have a grand time in Jerusalem."

"Who would take care of the flocks? When our men go we do their chores for them."

"Then it's their turn to do ours," Janette said.

"That's not the way it works. The men plan to go."

But Maggie was determined. "One man from each family can stay to do the chores. We will prepare food for them to eat while we're gone. Let's make this the year for women."

"Why is it that I now understand why Edita says she doesn't dare tell you 'No'?"

Dora walked in just in time to hear Nanette's rhetorical question. "Maggie doesn't give up easily."

"She won't take 'No' for an answer," Leora agreed. "She has an answer for everything."

Dora sat and reflected in a rocking chair while they worked. Maggie's determination and persistence in getting things done would be valuable tools in fulfilling her destiny with Jesus. ~She has an answer for everything, a wonderful quality for a teacher, if the answers were truth and not concocted only to have a reply. How will Maggie get her answers? We'll find out as life unfolds won't we? ~

The women of the two families met for a couple of hours each day to write to Edita and Nanette's Essene friends. Maggie and Deborah, Sarina and Janette copied them neatly and took them to the caravan station for delivery.

The days passed quickly while they prepared their clothes and readied provisions for the journey. Tents in case of rain, foodstuffs, water skins. One day, as they worked, Maggie reflected on how wonderful it was that their friends could read the letters. Few women could read and write. The other girls and mothers in Magdala did not learn.

"Mother, why is it that you and your friends from Heaven read and write though most women can't?"

"It was an educational community. We lived to walk with God and read inspirational writings in Hebrew, Greek, Aramaic, and Sanskrit. It was easy for me as my father, Apsafar, had Greek ancestors. We maidens shared our insights and wrote them down to review and teach others. We were able to set aside time for that because we shared the chores. Living in a community like that, everyone shared the same interest in spiritual growth."

"The head woman, Judy, taught that a new age is dawning and believed in teaching women. If you teach girls, you reach their future families. It's how she prepared us for the time to come. She wanted us to extend waves of intelligence and make a difference."

"Is that the reason you all left?"

"Yes, we went there to learn and left to apply it and teach others.

"There were only men in the Essene community until a brilliant leader believed that women must be involved if the Essene philosophy were to have an impact beyond Mount Carmel. Then his wife was to have a son to follow in his footsteps. To their surprise, the Lord sent them a female child instead. She was named Judy and grew to lead the community."

"How did you learn about Essenes?"

"Judy stayed at our inn in Bethlehem on the way to Jerusalem to visit her brother. She became my teacher because she saw that I was sincere about my walk with God and heard me say that some of the things in the Bible didn't make sense to me. My sister, Sarapha, was also sincere, but was less interested in mysticism. Judy searched for young women to come to Mount Carmel and learn the Essene way of thinking and living. My mother, Sodaphe, believed it an opportunity for me to escape the subservient life of women in Bethlehem. She didn't want that for me. I seized the opportunity. And she allowed me to go with tears in her eyes. Nanette went for the same reasons. We thought we might meet enlightened men who would share our beliefs."

"And it worked for you. You and Nanette met Papa and Jonathan."

Edita smiled, reflecting on her experience. "Wouldn't it be great if we could encourage other women and girls to read and write when we go to Jerusalem?"

"Do your experiences in Heaven explain why you and Papa let me play stickball with the boys?" Maggie asked.

"We had reservations about that. We've kept our beliefs to ourselves, lived accordingly, and set an example for our children. Your penchant for playing stickball attracts attention, especially since you are good at it. But I think your stirring to play cannot be denied and I'm sure something good comes of it in the big scheme of things. We'll know what that is by the time you are my age."

Edita gave a short laugh. "Even though it is unusual, I don't think it harms anyone."

"Do you think everyone knows that we read and write?"

"Maybe a few. We haven't made a big deal of it. When Deborah comes, you sometimes read, but you don't read when Lizette is around, just because she doesn't."

"Do you think Lizette is smart enough to read?"

"Of course. She just hasn't had the opportunity. Humanity is becoming more enlightened. There will come a time when everyone will read. I've taught you, Leora, and Sarina. You will teach your children. By the time you leave our loving household, it will be less unusual for women to read, write, and discuss writings. You have an inquisitive mind and will be a great teacher. You're a wonderful leader too. You've managed to make all the women in Israel eager to go to Jerusalem."

Maggie perked up. "I have? How do you know?"

Edita pulled out a pile of letters. "These are from women who received our letters. They're coming."

"Is Jesus' mother coming? I want to meet Mary."

"Yes, here's a letter from her. Jesus was already insisting that she go. Our letter clinched it for her and she's bringing many other women from Nazareth. She wrote her sister, Salone, who is coming from Cana. My sister, Sarapha, is coming from Bethlehem. Mary's brother Simon's wife Josada invited us to stay with them in Bethany. I've heard from Elizabeth, Suzannah, Joanna, and Diana. They all wrote letters to other friends. You've caused a movement, Maggie."

Maggie danced around the room, exhilarated with excitement. She stopped to ask Edita, "Do Leora and Nanette know?"

"Nanette probably got other letters. I'm sure she knows."

"I'm going to go find out." She skipped to Nanette's.

Edita smiled and laughed affectionately to herself. ~And I thought I was going to ask her to go talk to Nanette.

~Too late.

~I love my irrepressible daughter.~

Enoch and his family journeyed south on the western shore of the Sea of Galilee passing Tiberias and the tropical Jordan valley. Though Maggie had lived by the Sea of Galilee all of her life, she had never been away from Magdala and was fascinated by the winding Jordan River with its glistening waters that rippled as it flowed down to the Dead Sea. There were lush fields of grain and pink oleander dotted the countryside. Majestic Mount Hermon was behind them to the north with its white, snow-capped peak. They camped under the stars.

Maggie urged Edita to watch for her friends.

"Who will take the same road we do on the way to Jerusalem?"

"Elizabeth won't. She'll come from Hebron, south of Jerusalem. Neither will Saraphe from Bethlehem. Mary's sister Salone will go from Cana to Nazareth and travel with Mary and Joseph. We could see them when we get to the Valley of Jezreel. We'll meet Josada in

Bethany. She's invited the Essene sisters and their families to stay the night before Passover. You'll enjoy staying there. She has two children close to your age, Lazarus, Martha, and a baby, Mary."

Maggie was excited on the second day. When they reached the Valley of Jezreel, she looked for Jesus and his father, Joseph. She could think of nothing better than to see Jesus again.

They passed Ramath and Mount Gilboa loomed ahead. Their road would meet the one from Nazareth at Beth-shean.

"Mother, can we wait here for Mary, Jesus, and Joseph?"

"Better not. We don't know if they have already passed here or if they're still on the road west of us. See that mount ahead? That's Mt. Gilboa. There is a spring in the valley below it where we will spend the night. When we're settled there, we'll have time to look around for friends."

Maggie hoped Jesus was neither too far ahead nor too far behind for them to walk together. "Mother, there are a lot of people on the road today."

"Yes, more and more will join us on the road. Many celebrate Passover at the Temple in Jerusalem. We'll be engulfed by the crowd."

Maggie hoped she could find Jesus in the growing sea of humanity.

The men carried the best of their harvests of grain, fruit, and vegetables in white baskets or containers of gold and silver that they would offer in the Temple. Flutes played and the crowd sang Psalms of Ascents as they walked energetically down the road.

The weather was beautiful, neither too warm nor too cold. They removed their outer garments to feel the soft breeze and the damp coolness exuded by the Jordan.

Edita was lost in her own train of thought remembering their days at Mount Carmel where she had been dedicated to the Essene brotherhood by her parents. Other girls, consecrated by their own parents, learned the ways, mysteries, and understandings vital to the coming era. They were considered equals with the men in their mystical abilities to think, create, magnetize, and radiate the light of God. Twelve girls were chosen to be channels, to know truth so thoroughly that they could be moved by the Holy Spirit.

She recalled the day when she ascended the steps that led to the altar with the other maidens wearing their white linen robes, just as they had every day, to pray and burn incense. But that day, the child, Mary, was in the lead. The sun's morning light beamed strong from the east, clothing them in purple and gold robes of light. It cast shadows against the massive stone steps of the Essene temple as they mounted them. It was a clear day without a cloud in the sky, but when Mary reached the top step, there was thunder and lightning. Then the angel Gabriel took Mary's hand and led her to the altar. From this, the initiates knew that Mary was chosen to be the open door for the entrance of the Holy One into the world. He would bring an awakening to its people in preparation for the new era. They solemnly bowed their heads, consecrating themselves to assist in the service. Henceforth, they referred to that experience as The Dedication Ceremony.

Edita remembered waking in the middle of the night and hearing a low murmur of voices through the screens that afforded a modicum of privacy. She arose to assure herself that the child, Mary, was all right. She thought it strange that light showed between the panels. Looking around the panel, she saw four-year-old Mary watching the Archangel Michael direct small angels dressed as toy soldiers to march forward and back to teach her the activities of defending angels. She asked the little girl about them the next day. Mary told her that the live dolls acted out stories for her.

Edita's attention returned to the present as the crowd started the Psalms of Degrees. They soon came to the spring and prepared their evening's repast.

Maggie spied Jesus across the meadow and rushed to meet him. They hugged and whirled around together, laughing the way they had when they first discovered they would be friends. When they were dizzy, they staggered crazily and fell to the ground, out of breath, giddy with joy.

Not wishing to lose sight of Maggie, Edita had followed her. She heard a voice, "Edita!"

"Mary!" She rushed to give her old friend a hug. They hadn't seen each other since their days in the Heaven community at Mount Carmel. Mary had been one of the younger initiates, much advanced for her age. Edita helped her orient to the communal way of life. "I've been so excited knowing that I would see you again. Of course, I've had news of you through Joseph and Jesus. Jesus is growing into a fine young man."

"Yes, and I see he has a cute young friend." She smiled, laughter in her eyes. "Would you know anything about that, Edita?"

"That's my youngest daughter. She's your namesake, Mary. Come over here, Maggie."

Maggie came running, still flushed with excitement.

"She's Mary of Magdala, called Mary Magdalene, shortened to Maggie.

"Maggie, this is Mary, the mother of Jesus and wife of Joseph."

Maggie had never seen such kind eyes. She flung herself into Mary's arms and Mary welcomed what she thought would be a childish embrace. But it was intense, magnetic, Maggie holding on passionately and Mary unwilling to let go. It seemed to Edita they had become glued together. Overcome with emotion, tears welled up in Maggie's eyes. After a prolonged hug, she looked up into Mary's, surprised to see her eyes were also filled with tears. Maggie held on to Mary's shoulders and Mary stroked her hair. "I see that we have a special relationship, Maggie. We will do wonderful things together."

They loosened their embrace and sat on a rock, cuddled together, tears flowing with the realization of perfect love. Edita and Jesus looked on, also feeling the waves of love and holding the light for them.

When the mood subsided, Maggie turned to face Mary. "I'm so glad to meet you, Mary. I've wanted to meet you since I met Jesus. I love you, Mary."

Mary was equally moved. She laughed affectionately, giving Maggie a squeeze. "I know. I love you too."

She turned to Edita, "I hope you and Enoch will bring your family to eat with us."

The two families came together for supper of bread, cheese, fruit, and wine. As the evening ensued, other Essene friends joined them. Maggie, Jesus, and the other children formed a game of stickball. With Jesus's urging, Maggie took her place as pitcher and he positioned himself behind the hitter to catch her balls.

Mary said to Edita, "Let's go watch the game. I think I need to learn more about your youngest daughter."

As they watched the game, Edita told her that Maggie was the one who came up with the idea of bringing out the women, of her love of animals, her compassion for people, and her attraction to healing. "She spends a lot of time with Dora, our local healer."

This interested Mary, for she also had a passion for the healing arts. "She helps Dora a lot?"

"Yes, when she's not at her house tending the herb garden and preparing concoctions, she follows her on her rounds."

"How old is Maggie? She looks young to be interested in such serious pursuits."

"I agree. She's almost eleven. Remember when we were preparing for the new era at Mount Carmel? I wondered why I was there. No Archangel came with live dolls to cavort on my bed. I didn't have your clairvoyance and healing talents, Nanette's closeness to the nature kingdom, or Elizabeth's wisdom. I knew I could help the movement by cooking. It was the least I could do. So I did."

"Yes, you did. Cooking is also a God-given talent, Edita. And you were my guardian who raised me from the time my mother and father, Anna and Joachim, left me on the steps of the Essene temple. You read to me in Greek, Hebrew, Aramaic, and Sanskrit. I'll never forget you assisting the midwife at Jesus' birth. You and your Father were wonderful to arrange that private area in the cave behind the stable for us." She turned to face Edita. "You're important to my life."

"Thank you, but anyone could have done those things. Now I think my real reason for being at Mount Carmel was to learn how to teach Maggie. I feel that she will have an important role in establishing the new dispensation."

"I think you're right. As you saw, the magnetism I have with her is tremendous. I've never had such a strong feeling of recognition with anyone."

"I wonder if you're going to work together in some way."

"We'll see how it turns out. Time will tell."

They nodded together knowing that it was a blessing not to know more than they needed to know for each moment in their earthly sojourn. In the pageant they were playing out, now was the only time that counted.

Mary's eyes swept the playing field. "There are a lot of girls in the crowd because they know that we are making this the year for women, but I notice that Maggie's the only girl playing stickball."

"Look at them. They're cheering her on."

"Amusing. Little do they know that they are cheering their leader."

Edita was startled, "Their leader?"

"Of course. You said the women's movement was her idea."

Edita pondered this realization, "She's her own person. She doesn't do something just because others are. Neither does she not do something because others do not."

Mary nodded in approval, "I see that's true. Neither does Jesus."

"How does that play out?"

"It makes him different. He was teased and bullied."

"Did he defend himself?"

"Passively. He is immensely confident. He looks them squarely in the face and doesn't back down. They see he isn't afraid and that stops them. He laughs and makes a clever comment, and they relax their aggression. Our neighbor's son, Jacob, is his best friend. Jacob's good with his fists and has been known to intervene when Jesus was attacked. Those things seldom happen now. Jesus has learned to conceal things that might cause him to seem different from his peers."

"Are the bullies popular?"

"No, not really. They have their own group of insecure boys who think they are better if they put others down."

"I guess Jesus has a group? Not just Jacob?"

"Oh yes. There's a group of seven who have philosophical ideas and enjoy studying. Rabbi Barachia encourages original thinking. When they were younger, children gathered around Jesus because he was fun. He made whimsical and creative games. Actually, he still does. Little children are drawn to him."

"It sounds like he's the one who's popular. Independent and well liked. You've done a wonderful job with him."

Mary accepted Edita's praise matter-of-factly with a satisfied nod. "And you've done a wonderful job with Maggie."

They cheered as Jesus ran across home plate. Edita felt a sense of de ja vu, as if she had practiced this scene in the etheric realms during sleep. "It's surreal, isn't it? To be doing such mundane things while knowing the inner and spiritual undercurrents? It makes watching a children's stickball game seem insignificant."

Their two families were never very far apart the rest of the way to Jerusalem. On the second day, they passed the confluence of the tributary, River Jabbok, and the Jordan.

Jesus walked beside Maggie, "When I was eight, I told my Mother that I wanted to go from Jewry land and meet my kin in other countries of my heavenly Father's land. I don't believe God is partial to the Jews. We aren't more special than other people as Rabbi Barachia taught. The Jews built a wall around themselves trying to keep others out of the kingdom of our Father-Mother God."

He passed a palm branch to her. "I spent a year at the temple in Jerusalem when I was ten."

"How did you get to do that?"

"I got the attention of the chief of the Sanhedrin. It started when I saw butchers kill lambs and birds on the altar in the temple. The lambs were afraid. They didn't understand why man made them for such a senseless ending. Their despair moved me to appeal to our heavenly Mother and Father and I was naïve enough to believe I could talk to the perpetrators and save those innocent, loving animals.

"I asked the priest, 'Why?' He said it was a sacrifice to blot out our sins. I was appalled at this terrible misuse of God's energy and substance. The whole custom should be etherealized and returned to the light. We should use our powers of thought and feeling to manifest more appropriate offerings.

"In Jewish tradition, both David and Isaiah said it was a sin to bring burnt offerings before God. It fills the Temple with low vibrations. All sounds from a 'Home' of God should bring His glory into manifestation. Animals crying in despair and protest put a pall on the atmosphere. Only fools could think it impresses a loving God. I don't even think it impresses a loving person. How macabre!

"I was not even bar mitzvah and the priest thought me presumptuous to challenge the Law of Moses and temple practices. He took me before Hillel, chief of the Sanhedrin. I defended the bleating lambs and fearful doves and lamented the mortifying stench of their burning flesh. All odors in the Temple should be pleasant and add to the glory of God on earth. How can a God of love require such cruelty? I told him I wanted a God of love.

"Fortunately, he too wanted a God of love. He said, 'Come with me and we'll go find the God of love together.' I asked him why we needed to go anywhere when we could purify our hearts of cruelty and our minds of wicked thought to make within ourselves a temple for the God of love to dwell. 'Once we've prepared ourselves for

Him, he is there.' That impressed him and he asked my parents' permission for me to stay at the Temple to learn lessons from the Temple priests.

"My parents, especially my Mother, were thrilled that I was noticed."

Jesus fastened the center leaves of a palm frond together. "Hillel and I had lessons every day."

"And who was the teacher, you or Hillel?"

He smiled wryly, "Okay. I admit that I didn't hold back when I had something profound to say."

"While you were there, did you have any other experiences with the animals?"

"I rose early and communed with them. They are incredibly intelligent, unfettered with worldly desires. They are embodied elemental spirits who take form to serve humans who are in dense physical form and cannot see spirit bodies. Elementals sacrifice their spiritual freedom to serve the demands of humanity. Some are disenchanted with man and rebel with mischievous tricks, disasters, destructive lightning, and tornadoes. I've heard of storms at sea and tsunamis in distant oceans; earthquakes in Greece, volcanoes that spout fire and hot molten lava in Italy. Fallen ancient man feared these phenomena, thought they were acts of angry Gods who were scaring or punishing them.

"Men did not understand that they caused the disturbances with their own turbulent emotions and ignorant perceptions and continued to precipitate those events by fearing and resisting them. They projected those perceptions and emotions outward onto the stage of Earth then blamed the outcome on God. Man must understand that elemental life responds best to sharing and listening with feelings of love, peace, caring, forgiveness, and joy and thoughts of beauty, truth, purity, reverence, and respect for God's life flowing through all."

He wove the palm fronds into a circular shape.

"I appreciated Hillel's love and openness in discussing God, but was honestly glad to leave the oppressive practices of the Temple."

They camped near Mount Sartaba that night. The third day, they made their way to Jericho where they stayed and walked through the ruins of the old city.

A continuous flow of travelers filled the road on the fourth and last day of the trip. Most were on foot, some on donkeys or horses. Maggie and Jesus could tell from occasional splotches of camel dung that there was a caravan ahead.

They saw the mountains across the Jordan and the listless water of the Dead Sea when they climbed the hills leading to Jerusalem. They stopped on the eastern slope of the Mount of Olives near the small village of Bethany where Simon, Josada, and their three children had invited them to refresh before pressing on.

A tingle rippled through Maggie's body at the splendor before them when they looked down on the Holy City of Jerusalem from the top of the Mount of Olives. Maggie had never dreamed of such a great city. The inspiring symmetry of the Temple on Mount Moriah gleamed from the light of the sun and was the first thing she noticed, its imposing grandeur dwarfing even the pretentious palaces spread around it like hand maidens surrounding a queen.

Her excitement grew as they entered the city teaming with throngs of people. There was too much to take in. People looked like ants in comparison to the huge palaces. She stared as she passed the Temple, unable to take her eyes away. Edita resorted to holding her hand to keep her from getting lost. Maggie was so distracted she didn't even think to protest this childish treatment.

Mary's wealthy uncle, Joseph of Arimathea, had offered to house the families of the Essene women in his compound. It was a marble structure, elaborately furnished. It had fine hangings and a beautiful garden in the interior court. They arrived on Thursday to rest and prepare the Passover celebration.

The women rose on Friday with big plans. They bustled about Uncle Joseph's kitchen to bake bread, wash vegetables and fruit, and prepare desserts. They rested next to a spraying fountain under olive trees between flowers, vegetables, and herbs with exotic birds cawing and preening in the garden. This estate concealed and protected them from the outside mob where the poor begged, whores paraded their wares, and sellers hyped their goods. It was peaceful in Uncle Joseph's home and garden. What a wonderful place for the women to plan their activities!

CHAPTER 6

The women's meeting was a wonderful opportunity for them to gather in one place. They shared things from their localities and decided how to help each other.

They divided into groups of four or five and revealed their joys and concerns. A spokeswoman from each group gave a summary of their discussion.

The women adhered to the Essene way of life with varying levels of consistency. It was much easier for those who were married to men of the Brotherhood[1], even less difficult if they lived near other Essene families.

A few were ridiculed for their sincere beliefs and different way of living. They discreetly kept their unusual way of living secret by blending into the lifestyles of the communities where they lived. Not all were able to stay close to nature as Enoch and Edita did. Some of the maidens were from wealthy and privileged families and had gone back to take responsibility for large households in sprawling cities.

Most could say that they influenced others by their way of life and all were able to educate their children in reading and writing Hebrew, Sanskrit, Aramaic, and Greek. Clearly they were not establishing an earthly kingdom, but were expanding God's kingdom on Earth.

Their difficulties stemmed from their own desire to share their teachings. They were enthusiastic about what they knew and wanted to shout it from the rooftops, but success depended on discretion.

Each cluster of women divulged that it was difficult to find appropriate mates for their children. Edita was concerned because her son, Dan, was not yet married and Sarina was of age, but had little prospect of finding a husband.

---

[1] meaning Essene Brotherhood.

The women returned to their clusters and found ideas and solutions to help each other as life went forward.

They would share with the traditional women in their communities in subtle ways. They encouraged each other to keep their own counsel about their efforts to usher in the next age, to give information only when someone asked questions that indicated they had the expanded awareness needed to accept Essene knowledge. They wanted to share, but also avoid the backlash caused from giving unwelcome information.

There were two viewpoints about finding appropriate mates. Children might bring others in if they married outside the brotherhood, but they were more likely to pass the wisdom to the next generation if their life partners were also Essene.

Each woman stood to announce the gender and age of their marriageable children and give their place of abode.

As Edita rose to declare, she had misgivings. If Sarina married into a family far away, it would be necessary to part with her because she would leave Magdala to live with her husband's family. She announced Sarina anyway because she knew Sarina would be happier in an Essene family than in a traditional one.

She didn't announce Maggie as she was underage, but if Maggie also left Magdala to start a family of her own, Edita and Enoch would be left with Dan, Leora, and their spouses. Thank God that Leora was already established and happy in Magdala. But life went on. There would be grandchildren that she could teach the Essene knowledge and ways.

There was a special meeting of the twelve maidens that were trained at Mount Carmel. They were anxious to hear from Mary about the child of promise. She told the story of meeting Joseph, becoming pregnant and traveling to visit Elizabeth. Elizabeth told about her son, John. Edita helped describe Jesus' birth.

They learned of Mary, Joseph, Jesus, Elizabeth and John's escape to Egypt and their studies in Luxor and Alexandria. Mary and the maid, Josie, had stories to tell of their education and the boys' childhood.

The maidens were gratified that all was going as planned with Jesus and showered Mary with blessings and offers to help. She took information on their locations so that she could depend on them when the time came for action in their regions.

Edita was amazed how the brotherhood was dispersed throughout Israel. They had at least one friend in every geographical area. This was a strong network. Holy Spirit had placed them strategically.

"Jesus, what is the best thing about your visit to Jerusalem?"
"Seeing you."
"Thank you." Maggie skipped over the amenities. "I'm glad to see you too. What else?"
"Seeing Lazarus, Martha, and Mary and staying at their house in Bethany. Their father, my uncle Simon, generously allowed me to stay with them, even after my parents left for Nazareth."
"They are wonderful friends."
"I'm glad that Mother and other women from Nazareth came, but I'm sad that she went to the Court of Women and wasn't allowed to come into the Temple with us. Which reminds me, women aren't required to come. How did you manage it?"
"I insisted. Papa, Dan, and Samuel were going to come without us. But I got other women interested in coming. When the men were about to leave, we were packed and ready to go. They couldn't leave us there. They knew we would come anyway. How did your mother get to come?"
"I refused to come unless she did. When she decided to come, so did other women from Nazareth. There are an extraordinary number of women here this time. Women from many villages felt inner stirrings to come. They are very intuitive. This is a special time for women, Maggie. Their role will change during the coming dispensation. You knew to come because you were tuned to the Divine Will.
"And I'm glad I did. The women are nothing to the leadership of Israel. They are only significant in their own households. In my family, my father and mother confer with each other and make decisions together."
Jesus nodded, "Mine as well."
"That isn't true of most families in Israel. You should hear the women talk. Women are only things to men, fit only to give them pleasure, have babies, and take care of them. Men regard them as possessions beneficial to them like sheep, goats, cows, and donkeys. They aren't allowed to learn to read and write."

"My Mother reads and writes and she taught me and my brothers and sisters," Jesus said. We brothers went to synagogue school. When we got home we taught our sisters."

"That's the way we did it in our home, but our family is smaller. We discussed Dan's lessons at the supper table, but look at that. Why should we girls have to stay home and get the lessons second hand? We only studied within our own families. It wasn't shared among friends, so I have friends who can't read and write. My sisters and I talk about the stories in the Bible and the writings of sages. We can talk with Deborah and Janette like that too because they read, of course, coming from an Essene family. Any philosophical discussions I have with Lizette are based on our observations of what we see. We talk about things, not ideas. Small wonder that women's conversation degenerates into gossip and judgmental back biting.

"In Magdala, women convene to sew and visit while men are away in the afternoon. During harvest, they gather to preserve fruit and grind grain. Sometimes they knead yeast bread.

"That's my relationship with Deborah. When we are together, we work on projects. We made a blanket together and we talk about things we've read. We can't talk like that when Lizette is with us. We have tea with Lizette and talk about how to fix her hair, how to wear her clothes. She's obsessed with my looks and tries to fix me. She talks about Raamah a lot. She has a crush on him and wonders if he likes her. She dreams about her wedding.

"All the girls I know, even Lizette, make things for their futures. They embroider pillow cases, towels, and table cloths. They make blankets, and weave rugs. In my family, we make pottery. Women are industrious. They are intelligent. How else could they organize their families, run households, and teach children what they need to know? They are seldom idle.

"When they prepare a feast, all assist. It is a social occasion that makes the work fast and easy."

Maggie warmed to the subject. "They plant gardens, watch them grow, weed them, and tend them. They gather vegetables, cook, and preserve them. They are very busy. For all of this, they are overlooked, considered dumb, and are discounted," she complained.

"Their ideas and opinions are seldom sought. They are very creative and expressive, but they are repressed in the community.

They are not allowed to speak in synagogue, not even allowed to read from the writings.

"Men think women are helpless. They think I am an anomaly because I tend animals, play sports, and stand up to men. Even women think that about me because they don't do it. Men in most towns think that healers have to be men and priests. If it weren't for Dora, they would think that in Magdala.

"Men brag about their accomplishments: about battles, sports, fishing, tending sheep, killing predators. I've overheard stable hands boast about their sexual exploits with whores and wives. I guess all men do that. For all I know, the men who associate with my father and brother do that too. They are just careful not to talk when women are around so I haven't heard them."

Jesus was fascinated by her ribald honesty. Other girls didn't talk so openly.

Maggie remembered what he had said at the beginning of the conversation. "Jesus, I got carried away. What did you mean about this being a special time for women? What will their new role be?"

He sat his cup down quietly, gave her a smug smile, and said mildly, "I think that's up to you."

They walked through the market with its silks, spices, and food stuffs, letting their eyes rove over the musical instruments, hand hewn furniture, and delicate crafts.

"Oh, Maggie?"

"Yes."

"That bragging you heard in the stables? Their stories aren't true."

It took her a moment to catch on to his sly humor. Then she remembered her remark about the sexual exploits and broke out in wild laughter.

Later, Maggie walked by the temple and saw Jesus talking to priests and doctors. He declared that it was the time for prophecy to come to pass. "Israel sets itself above God. Priests, doctors, and lawyers live in luxury while they oppress the poor. Your offerings are abominations. God only wants the service of self to love and light. He does not require sacrifices. Israel must return to the truth of its wholeness and manifest peace, love, joy, wisdom, and forgiveness. I warn you, soon foreign nations will overcome Jerusalem and tear down the Temple. But the time is coming when people will dwell in peace together. Each person's inner Christ will manifest and the I AM presence of God will reign within each soul."

Ignoring the insulted look on the faces of the priests, he walked away, leaving them to contemplate his words. In so doing, he caught sight of Maggie near the balustrade. He motioned her to walk beside him and they entered the mass of humanity, alone together in the crowd.

"Those were bold words. Are you declaring yourself?"

"No, my time has not yet come."

"Do you know when that will be?"

"I must wait for my destiny to unfold. If I spent more time here, the priests in the Temple would be very uncomfortable before my time. There's no more to say to them now. I have lived with the traditional idea of truth for thirteen years. Now I know that even priests in Jerusalem put themselves in a prison of their own making with earthly laws and taboos that block true unity with the Christ living within them. Not only that, they force people to live by false laws. Just two days ago, they killed a gentile who accidentally wandered into the court of Israel.

"Have you seen that placard on the entrance to the Court? Here's what it says:

Let no stranger enter within the balustrade
and the enclosing wall around the sanctuary.
Whoever may be caught, shall blame himself for his certain death.

I swear to you that I will someday tear down that obscenity."

He passionately objected to ostracism of gentiles in the Temple. Maggie waited for him to calm down.

He continued, "I asked many questions this week, but priests can only parrot back what is written in the Torah. They have no profound answers like my friends and I who were inspired with the tutelage of Rabbi Barachia in Nazareth.

"Nazareth is very liberal."

"That is due to the influence of visitors who travel through Nazareth on the way to lands beyond. Many spend time there and come to synagogue. Barachia invites foreign philosophers, priests, and teachers to speak there."

"Can't you just tell the Temple priests what they need to know?"

"It's casting pearls before swine. They do not see the value. Hillel is fascinated by my words and encourages me. Others are jealous and think it presumptuous of me, a mere lad, to speak in the Temple. No. I can only ask questions now, but I can be like Socrates and ask them in such a way that they draw the correct conclusions. And when I read, I can choose scripture that says what I want to say and comment on it in the context of today."

"When scholars come through Nazareth, what do you learn from them?"

"Enough to know that I can learn more. I want to go to Greece and hear the Oracle, to learn from the Brahmins and Buddhists in India, and the Masters in Tibet. I want to visit the Magi and study the Avesta[1] in Persia."

He faced her. "Let's travel together, Maggie, and learn how all of God's children are inspired by Spirit and allow God to live through them. There is much that is not available in Israel. It's impossible to get it here because the Jews isolate themselves from others."

"You're right. If we could obtain such writings, we might be ostracized for studying them. Even the Essene way is looked at askance, but travel is acceptable for commerce and trade."

"We could travel with caravans to the Orient, live in that culture, and study their writings. There are as many customs as there are countries. I want to experience all walks and ways of life so I can understand people's thoughts, feelings, and needs, and help them."

"Do you think all people need to learn the same thing?"

"Basically, yes. All know a small portion of the truth of God. But all need to learn the whole truth to achieve oneness with the All in All."

"After we've gone to other lands, we'll see if this is where God calls us to make changes," Maggie said.

"It must be. After all, we took the robe of earth in this location. Our hearts stir for more. Our guidance leads us to explore."

"We will go. We'll know it is time when the excitement of our inner urges can no longer be suppressed."

They clasped hands and looked into one another's eyes. "We will travel the earth together."

---

[1] the collection of sacred texts of Zoroastrianism.

And thus their pledge was made. The die was cast. Destiny spoke the word through them. They went their separate ways until God summoned them to activate their calling.

Here we are on our way. Our forerunners have trained our protagonists.
Our main players are together.
It's too soon. We must split them.
They are Divine Complements, created as one. No matter how much space we put between them, they attract like magnets.
Why not let them grow together?
They must develop apart from each other.
Why?
She's a female. He is male. If they develop together, she will be his shadow and will never know herself. She will only know him. We've seen it many times.
True. That's only one reason that Divine Complements seldom embody together.
I have an idea. Magnets have a limited field of attraction. If they are far enough apart, they won't attract.
These might. Have you checked their auras? They are the most intense incarnated on earth today.
They are so strong that the ultimate success of the mission is certain when they are brought together.
That's true . . . , unless they waste it on excessive worldly pleasures.
Is that even possible?
We've seen that too. The earth's illusion is mighty in its allure. Many a pilgrim has succumbed to its charms.
The danger is great. It is the most devious succubus in the universe. If they use their powers for personal gain, our mission is doomed to failure.
But when they remember to use their incomparable power in service to God, the One in All, and stay in balance as they serve others, they will succeed.
Divine Instruments come forth into the world, to transform the world. The transformation must come through embodied souls. Fulfilling themselves on our side will not affect the earth. It's their mission to anchor the masculine and feminine.
Noted, and agreed. But the poles of their energy must be balanced. The feminine must equal the masculine.
You know the trouble we've had when masculine dominates. It results in violence, devious greed, vengeful judgment, selfishness, conceit, and limitation. Arrogant use of force manipulates, threatens, or intimidates. It stifles kindness and understanding.
The feminine nature is not blameless in this dynamic. It confounds the problem with false humility. It surrenders to demands with disdain, submits reluctantly without devotion. It grows indifferent, cajoles with flattery, or

manipulates. It allows itself to be gullible instead of maintaining clarity and responding honestly. When it doesn't understand, it rationalizes. When it loses respect, it reacts with deceit, rebellion, and acquiescence instead of loyalty. Therefore, there is reticence to dominance instead of balance; distrust instead of faith; and suspicion instead of forgiveness.

The masculine can become lost in the material pleasures or make the feminine afraid, thus causing it to hide or flee. Eventually, this accumulates, resulting in hopelessness.

Her energy must match his. An excess of power can result in greed, war, waste, cruelty, promiscuity, prejudice, suspicion, and deceit. Let them grow separately. Then they will unite in a powerful dynamic climax.

When?

When?

When will they unite?

Near the end.

But they need time together to practice their synergetic energy, to prepare for the end.

Reluctantly, I agree. How can we assure they are consecrated to their Divine Purpose?

Impress their minds. Give them temptations and trials. Initiate them when they overcome. Make them cognizant of the mission's importance. The mission must supersede every personal desire.

They will deny themselves.

But they are lovely and pure. They have earned fulfillment.

Let them 'fulfill' themselves when they return to us. They can't achieve complete oneness anyway while their physical bodies block their portals to the soul.

That's true, but remember: self, time, and space are not real. They only seem to exist in the earthly illusion. Therefore, there are ways to achieve oneness, even for the earthbound.

This I've got to see.

Fine. We'll let them demonstrate for you. Divine Instruments come forth in the world, to transform the world. The transformation must come through embodied souls.

Coherently Connected Divine Consciousness[1] sounded her keynote of spiritual freedom.

Eternal co-creation.

---

[1] Also called 'higher realms of light,' 'together standing in the light,' 'oneness,' 'holographic synchronicity,' 'Divine Collective.'

CHAPTER 7

On the way home from Jerusalem, Edita told Maggie about delivering Jesus in the stable behind her father's inn in Bethlehem.

"The city was crowded with descendants of David who were there to be counted by the Romans. Mary's delivery time was imminent. She thought it propitious that Joseph happened to be going to Bethlehem at that time. We were friends since our time at Mount Carmel and she wanted me to deliver her Son. She loved and trusted me and I knew the Essene ritual for delivery.

"Joseph and my father, Apsafar, were fellow Essenes. The two of them knew a place away from the throng and hidden from the prying eyes of Romans. A grotto was tucked behind the inn stable, barely noticeable to those who stabled their horses and donkeys there, and there was a direct path to it from our family kitchen.

"My mother, Sodaphe, called us girls to ready the cave room for Mary and Joseph. When she told me who was coming, my blood boiled with excitement, knowing that the glorious event we had prepared for was taking place and I would be there. I found Mary as soon as your aunt, Sarapha, and I finished mucking out the stable next to the cave and moved the animals away. That part of the stable would be available for visitors from the Brotherhood and others who knew of the impending birth. I summoned Margil, the midwife, who stayed at our inn, for she was also there to be counted. She had delivered Elizabeth's son, John, and through the divine feminine principle of synchronicity, was present in Bethlehem. When I found her, she was happy to see me. We had been together at Mount Carmel and were good friends. I didn't hesitate. 'Mary and Joseph are here. She's about to have her firstborn.' Her eyes were wide with joy. She grabbed her bag of birthing supplies and followed me to the garden grotto.

"This was the moment we had been waiting for, our reason for studying with Judy in Mount Carmel, Gabriel's reason for announcing Mary as the mother of the Messiah, our parents' reason for dedicating us for training by the Essene Brotherhood, our reason for marrying within the Brotherhood, and for leaving Mount Carmel. It was meant for us to be together for the birth. And Ceasar Augustus, an unwitting tool in the divine design, demanded that we be in Bethlehem. Even Roman rulers participated in the enactment of the birth. We thought it wonderful that the Divine Plan brought us together, so fond we are of one another.

"Your Grandmother Sodaphe, your Aunt Sarapha, Margil the midwife, and I got there quickly.

"It was an easy birth and I was the first to hold Jesus when he sprang from Mary's womb, kicking, and vocalizing. Whether his cries were of joy at such an accomplishment or showed fear upon entering a cold world, it's hard to say. But there is no doubt that our tears, commingled with laughter and wonder, were of happiness too great to be told. Blissful! Jubilant! Euphoric!

"His miniature hands and feet enthralled me and his small fuzzy head felt delightful. I gazed at his tiny features in wonderment.

"It wasn't until my eyes settled on the opening and closing of his mouth that I remembered what I was supposed to do. The sweet little child wanted to suckle. I gently laid him next to Mary's breasts. They rested peacefully while I removed the soiled linens. Margil cut the cord then Sarapha laid him on the manger beside the pitcher and bowl that Mother had brought from the kitchen. We washed him while his arms flailed and his legs pumped. Sarapha swaddled him in soft cloths and a sheepskin that a shepherd brought. She held him for a few moments before laying him beside Mary."

"Shepherd! What was a shepherd doing in the birthing chamber?"

"Well, you know, shepherds think that stables are their personal domain and they attend the birth of many lambs. He belonged there as much as we did. I think this particular one wanted to be close to this child who was special to him."

"It sounds like you know this shepherd. What was Jesus to him?"

"It was Mary's brother, Simon, who lives in Bethany."

"Oh! Simon and Mary must be very close. No wonder he found an excuse to come to the grotto!"

"The grotto was very comfortable. It is a lovely garden area with trees overhead, stones to sit on, and a manger where we fed farm animals that wander. You know how it is at our house. Our animals are part of our family. I believe that Mary and Joseph were very pleased with their accommodations, as pleased as we to have them as our guests.

"The inn was very busy, but we had workers to do everything and Essene brothers and sisters helped. Other guests were busy with their own family reunions and heedless of what we did. Few knew there was a birth."

"Did other Essenes come?"

"Yes, and other shepherds known to Simon. An inspired shepherd-musician, Eucuo, calmed the babe with harp and reed."

"Did they come because they were with Simon?"

"Some did. Other shepherds came because of inner sight, hearing, feeling, and knowing. Guidance led them to our cave. The ethers vibrated with celestial light and they heard whispers of peace and glory and felt an inner urge to come and honor Jesus."

"It must be a wonderful thing to follow inner urges."

"I think so. Magian priests who saw the birth written in the stars came from Persia. This led them to Jerusalem. They met Mary's cousin, Zacharias, there. He gave them directions to Bethlehem and they found the way to our inn. They arrived during Mary's confinement, but waited to see Jesus after her purification so we visited with them.

"They were interesting. They rode camels and brought gifts. Mer brought gold to symbolize material power, Hor brought frankincense for etheric wisdom, and Lun brought myrrh for healing. Body, mind, and soul, the three levels of human existence."

"What a big fuss! I've never heard of a birth attracting so much attention. Did shepherds and wise men come to visit me?"

"No, we were normal. Any birth is a wonderful thing."

"I know. And relatives love to see newborns. Everyone is proud of new babies. Too bad babies can't remember it. I guess that Mary and Joseph liked all the attention."

"I think that Mary did. She has high aspirations for Jesus to lead the Jews."

"I think he's a good leader. He is certainly smart and talented, but he's not a pretentious boy. Not like Raamah who will rule the synagogue. I don't think Jesus is the type to be a ruler."

"Mary told me that Joseph doesn't think so either. He thinks Jesus will be a great teacher and show humanity how to live."

"I think that sounds better. Who would want to be a ruler? Giving orders all the time, wearing bulky, rich clothing, never having any privacy, not knowing who your real friends are. It doesn't sound comfortable to me."

"Time will tell. We'll see how Jesus handles his notoriety."

Maggie went home with her family. It seemed incongruous to return to daily life after being to Jerusalem and its Temple. She was disappointed that such a magnificent edifice was the site of such ignominious actions.

Jesus would not come back to Magdala for a long time. He finished synagogue school in Nazareth. Now, she would not see him around Magdala every other month. He would take his place in a trade and wouldn't take vacations.

Maggie supposed Jesus would join Joseph's carpentry shop, but Joseph no longer had business in Magdala. Jesus loved his heavenly Father-Mother God and enjoyed discussing high ideals. He was uniquely suited for spiritual service, but he would have to marry before he could be a rabbi. Now, he would find a wife.

Thoughts of Jesus permeated her life. Everything stirred memories of times with him: Getting water at the well, tending the sheep, going to synagogue, fishing in the boat in the Sea of Galilee, playing stickball, resting in a cave, helping Dora, preparing food with Sarina and Edita, visiting with Leora, seeing her best friend, Deborah, and spending time with Jesus' uncle, aunt, and cousins. On and on and on.

She carefully hid her interest in him. She didn't ask his cousins what he was doing or where he was. They didn't hear from him either. It was a whole day's journey over hills to travel from Nazareth to Magdala, not a trip made frivolously.

The Essene way was not to magnify personal attachments. Though Essene initiates came together for that one Passover, their connection was a spiritual one. They were emotionally uninvolved. However, inspiration brought them together when needed.

Enoch and Edita thought Maggie was finally big enough to make pottery at the wheel. She helped Enoch for a few hours every morning. The earthy smell of the damp clay permeated the atmosphere. The whirring of the wheel as it rotated smoothly on its base filled the air with a steady hum. She helped him mix the clay, stir until it thickened, put it on the potter's wheel, and fashion circular shapes: plates, bowls, mugs, and pitchers.

Maggie found it fascinating to watch Enoch's dexterity at the wheel. He was totally absorbed in the process, so at one with the movement of the wheel and the transformation of the clay that he was mesmerized.

She never interrupted him when she brought him water and snacks. She patiently waited until he finished a piece to call his attention to the nourishing morsels. When she neglected to speak to him, she came back later to find the refreshments sitting, untouched, on the table beside him, so preoccupied was he in the production of stoneware.

Maggie didn't mind watching and waiting, for he was poetry in motion. No movement was wasted and there was no hesitation. When he worked at the wheel, his actions were continuous and had a repetitive rhythm.

Equally organized when he applied colored slips, he plied his stylus with precision, scraping tiny engravings that peeled shavings of clay in curls. He brushed off residue leaving smooth ridges and textures adding depth to the design. She loved the scorched dry smell when he bisque fired the pitchers and mugs. He efficiently waxed the underside of plates and saucers.

When he used the brush to add detail, he applied the exact pressure and amount of paint needed to shape designs in fluid motions. Three strokes in perfect precision each time he loaded the brush. He was a skilled artisan who made it look easy to practice his craft.

Enoch liked company while he worked. When at the wheel, he ignored all else, but enjoyed Maggie's presence when she watched. He talked companionably while making intricate designs with efficient brush or stylus strokes.

Maggie loved being in his studio. They were comfortable with silence, but didn't feel disturbed when the other talked. It was a communion of souls in shared thoughts. He often made remarks that were extensions of her thinking.

She asked him questions because she desperately wanted to know her father. He was often with other men, more comfortable around his son than his daughters. She wanted the same closeness with him as her brother Dan. She sometimes thought Enoch wasn't sure what to do with his girls. He undoubtedly loved them, but was slightly intimidated by their beauty and overwhelmed by their devotion.

She loved his responses to her questions. He would get a thoughtful look on his face, for her questions were seldom answerable with few words or short phrases. She would work quietly until he composed his thoughts on the matter and she listened attentively to his explanations.

Then her thoughts rolled, stimulated by his input. A few minutes later, she would follow up with a comment or question. Their conversation was continuous, but unhurried. Others walking into the shop would be unaware that they were communicating at all.

He allowed her to fashion clay animals and tiny furniture when she was small and fired them in the kiln with his orders. Now, at eleven, she made saucers and bowls, and learned to make them perfectly round, balanced, and symmetrical. This was the beginning of her marriage set. She worked on it at odd times and it would be finished when she was fifteen.

Marriage. She held all the boys she knew in disdain. Those from Magdala's 'best' families were arrogant and rude and she wanted nothing to do with them. The ones she teamed with in stickball were friends, nothing more or less. She wasn't attracted to Yaar, Enosh, Tobias, Aaron, or Barak in 'that' way. Even Jesus was only a good friend. Yaar was apprentice to Enoch and she was around him all the time, but he was like a brother, and she ignored him to go about her own business.

Oh well. It didn't matter whether she found anyone. She could live like Dora. Dora had a full life and she lived a single life. Maggie was inclined to spend as much time with Dora as possible.

Dan was marrying Leora's friend, Batia. She didn't have Essene training, but she was Leora's best friend and had participated in her wedding.

They did not weave, sew, garden, and collect nuts and honey like they did for Leora's wedding. Edita said that the bride's family was in charge of the wedding party and the feast. Leora would wear a special robe because of her place in the ceremony as Batia's closest friend. Edita, Sarina, and Maggie sewed special dresses for the occasion and outfitted Enoch and Dan in fine robes.

Dan, Enoch, and Samuel built a north wing to Enoch and Edita's compound for Dan to live with Batia. They would share meals, chores, and a common patio. The men were experienced carpenters now after building Samuel and Leora's house under Joseph's tutelage.

Maggie gladly welcomed Batia into the family. She was a skilled seamstress and did exquisite embroidery. Her family's philosophy wasn't as close to Enoch and Edita's as Jonathan and Nanette's, but she spent many days with them as Leora's friend. She knew their way of life and was delighted with its contrast to her traditional upbringing. She envied Leora for her closeness to her family and their relaxed, but devout way of living.

To Maggie, Dan was the most wonderful young man in the world. He would be a wonderful husband. Unlike other boys, he helped his mother with cooking and cleaning. Batia wouldn't have to pick up after him. He would help with the gardening. He would be a great father. Maggie had experienced his fatherly attributes when he taught her things. He was patient, caring, and a good listener. She hoped Batia appreciated him.

The wedding preparations were like those for Leora in many respects. Dan recited from scripture on the Sabbath and young girls showered him with nuts and fruit.

Maggie entered the bride's chamber with Edita and Sarina. They brought gifts and well wishes for Batia. The women and young girls sang together and the mothers gave advice to Batia.

The family took their place beside Dan in the ceremony and saluted the happy couple. During the feast, Maggie played the harp and sang with Sarina while Leora performed a passionate dance to entertain the couple. They participated when the young women of the village danced to the band and watched when the young men joined in an energetic hora. The bride and groom circulated to all the tables to greet their guests. Maggie and her sisters visited with each guest for a short time to make sure they had a good time and got involved in the entertainments.

Maggie celebrated her bat mitzvah when she was twelve and became a woman in the eyes of the world. She had anticipated this day all of her life. The family invited all their friends to her special ceremony. When Samuel played the opening song on his harp, Enoch presented her to the community as a woman. Touched by this experience and engulfed in the love of her father and the affection of the crowd, tears of joy welled up in Maggie's eyes. She dried her eyes with Edita's handkerchief when everyone applauded.

The family held great honor in Magdala and Maggie was highly regarded. The boys admired her pitching arm. She hoped they would still play stickball with her now that she was bat mitzvah.

Sarina loved to spin fiber into fine thread then dye and weave it into cloth on the large loom in the kitchen. She helped Edita cook and clean, but always had something on the loom that compelled her to finish it. When she spun, she couldn't stop what she was doing to help Edita lest the interruption make the thread uneven. She adeptly released the perfect amount of fiber into the spindle, gave it the exact tension needed to twist it into thin floss for fine weaving.

But when weaving, she could find a stopping place to help Edita with last minute meal preparations, take up the potatoes while Edita finished the sauce, and toss the vegetables while Edita carved the lamb.

Unlike Maggie, Sarina liked solitude. She was perfectly happy to weave in the kitchen while everyone else was on the patio singing together. Edita often reminded her to join the family.

Maggie grew to take the sheep to the fields alone with only Bo and Abbe for protection. As a precaution, she wore Dan's tunic and robe so strangers would think she was a boy. His clothes were masculine with dull colors of coarse cloth, unlike the more striking colors of fine fabric she wore in town. She strapped a dagger just above her knee, tucked a sling and stones of carved flint into one of the deep pockets in the lower sleeve. She put her lunch in the other side and carried a water vessel. She always had constructive things to do during her down time. Her harp hung on shoulder straps, a medium sized pouch held her embroidery and a stickball. The sheep took care of themselves. She only had to keep them calm, help with births, and watch for predators. Sometimes she played with the lambs or threw the ball for the dogs to chase.

Maggie walked beside Bessie at the head of the flock. Bo and Abbe guarded the sides and the rear. The big ram, Ephraim, walked majestically near Bessie.

Maggie remembered asking Dan why he named the ram after one of Joseph's sons. Dan had said, "I didn't really. I just named him what I wanted him to be. Ephraim means 'fruitful.' When he was born, I wanted him to sire many lambs, so I gave him a name that would build up his expectations."

Maggie laughed that he gave human qualities to a small lamb. Ephraim stayed busy. He often reared up on ewes as they grazed sedately in the pasture. The rest of the time he postured in a regal manner as if he ruled the universe.

She knew about sex and birthing while other girls did not. You learn a lot about life while in the pasture. The ewes looked uninterested and ignored Ephraim while he was conducting his business, but he was after them all the time. No wonder they were bored with him.

Maggie led the sheep to a lush field of grass and stowed her things under a tree. She collected a few rough stones to carry with her then stroked her harp and sang a peaceful song to lull the sheep into complacency. She played with the lambs. She fostered their affections from an early age so they cooperated when they were grown. Flocks who know their shepherdess trust her. Armed with her stickball and slingshot, she joined the cavorting lambs. She blended with them and tagged a young ram on the back then ran ahead to make him chase her. He caught up with her and playfully butted her side. She ruffled his head affectionately then put her attention on another.

A young ewe chased and leapt to catch a butterfly, but it eluded her. Maggie moved to distract her. Why did a baby sheep need a butterfly? She would only mangle it. Maggie sensed a stealthy movement out of the corner of her eye.

What was that? It was hard to tell, even when she looked directly at it. It blended with the rocks and sage. That couldn't be good. Anything moving warily was up to something. She slipped her sling and a flint rock out of her sleeve while she trained her eyes on the creature. It was wolf-like, too large to be a jackal, coyote, or fox.

She whirled the sling to give momentum to the stone and stared the creature in the eye. Bo and Abbe barked behind her.

"Heel!" They obediently sat on their haunches. The sling hurled the stone into the wolf's eye and it fell inert on rough gravel. She cut its throat to ensure it was dead.

She checked her flock. All was well. She finished her business with the wolf. She cut its skin around the ankles, turned it on its back, and made a deep stroke from its throat down the center of its torso. She stretched each leg one at a time and sliced through them from the paw to the core, then stripped the hide off the body, broke its neck, and cut through the sinewy muscles. She rolled the carcass into a ravine and spread the hide out in the sun next to the tree. She rinsed her hands and arms with water, sat down with her fruit, and assessed the situation.

Wolves run in packs so there were others close by. She had to protect her flock from vultures who would soon pluck the flesh off the wolf's bones. At least they wouldn't be tempted to prey on her lambs, not with a bloody, exposed carcass nearby to attract their attention. It was too early to go home, but she needed to alert other shepherds about wolves in the area.

She donned her supplies, whistled the gathering tones, walked toward Bessie and Ephraim, and headed toward the village with her charges.

Dan spied her rounding the curve. Sensing something was wrong, he rushed to meet her. Why did she bring the flock home so early? "Is everything all right? How are you?"

"A wolf came after the sheep."

"Are you sure it was a wolf? It could have been a fox or a jackal?"

"I know foxes and jackals." She lifted the wolf skin for him to see.

His face was grim, "It's a wolf all right."

Walking beside her, he mixed concern with admiration. "You killed it yourself." It was more a statement than a question. He knew her capabilities. "Maggie, I haven't even killed a wolf."

"You never needed to. You've killed jackals and foxes. I saw you do it."

"But a wolf! They're stronger."

She laughed sardonically, "Not when they're dead. I didn't have to wrestle it down. Slingshots and knives come in handy."

He laughed a ridiculous laugh. Her tension rolled away as she joined his laughter and tears of relief flowed down her face.

Hand in hand, they led the flock to the corral.

Everyone rushed out of the house and the shop to meet them. Dan lifted Maggie's hand in triumph and she raised the wolf hide with the other. The family's eyes went wide and mouths flew open. Bo and Abbe looked on, panting and energetically shifting their feet.

Edita threw her arms around Maggie, "Oh! My baby!"

Enoch held her protectively. Overloaded with a wolf hide, a harp, and a water vessel, in addition to the things in her pockets; Maggie almost collapsed under their embraces. Her siblings saw her dilemma. They took her things, ushered her inside to lunch, and urged her to tell the tale.

Edita shuddered when Maggie told of staring down the wolf. "If I had looked away, he would have attacked me."

Enoch wondered how she knew such things and realized her understanding came from instinct in the heat of experience.

"Why not bring the carcass home?" Sarina asked. "Papa and Dan would skin it."

"Hmmm. I could have, but I didn't think of that." She looked at her brother affectionately. "I was doing what Dan does. He skins the animals he kills. It was too heavy to carry home. I had to roll it over to skin it. It wasn't easy."

Really! Did she have to kill a wolf?

Of course she did. We're balancing the masculine and feminine energies of earth.

That doesn't mean we have to be destructive. It's an insult to assume the masculine is destructive.

Unfortunately, that is the way manhood is interpreted in the Earth illusion.

Ahem. Pardon me, but destruction is part of the cycle. When a personality, place, condition, or thing no longer serves the best interest of the divine collective, it must etherealize. It returns to its essence and re-forms into another manifestation that serves a new paradigm.

What purpose did the wolf serve? It destroyed innocent life.

We can't make rash statements. We consult the Akashic records to get the facts.

They calmed their mental and feeling worlds to tune to the frequency that resonates with the Book of Life.

Aha. Now we know the wolf was given to Earth as a totem to represent vengeful persons that manipulate the mass consciousness. It is a stalker that only hunts in a pack.

Why did it appear to the Magdalene? She isn't vengeful. Neither is she a stalker. She never manipulates and won't give her power away by depending on a pack.

Exactly. She can rule all those things out as they don't apply to her. Neither is the wolf a positive sign, so she can refuse to emulate it.

Then it is a warning to her personality from the astral world through her emotions. The wolf represents a person she will meet. Notice she overcame the wolf.

I understand. She will overcome the person.

CHAPTER 8

After Maggie washed and changed into her regular garb, they spread the news about the pack of wolves. Enoch and Dan visited people in the market and the women took their embroidery and sat in the shade by the well so people would talk to them. Everyone would know of the wolf sighting in just a few hours and take the necessary precautions.

Edita and Enoch decided not to reveal that Maggie was the one who found it and certainly didn't want anyone to know she killed and skinned it. Girls didn't do such things. It wasn't ladylike. Maggie would be of marriageable age soon and they must guard her future. News of such conquests might intimidate suitors.

Maggie had mixed feelings. She fought against shame, feeling she did something wrong that had to be hidden. She struggled with pride, wanting to show the wolf skin and bask in admiration. Dan was proud of her. Enoch was too, but he felt guilty that neither he nor Dan was there to protect her. Maggie thought that silly. If they were there, they would kill the wolf and she still wouldn't know she could defend herself. It was a heady feeling. She felt empowered. If she could kill a wolf, she could do anything. And now she sat here, doing embroidery, pondering how to make a coat of the wolf hide. There was balance in that.

"Maggie," Sarina gestured down the street, "Deborah's coming."

Deborah carried a wide jar crafted by Enoch. Seeing Maggie, she set her vessel down, pulled out her embroidery, and joined them. Soon they talked about the wolf sighting. Deborah's folks, being fisherman, never went to open pasture, but their families shared everything.

Soon Maggie saw Dora going home from a call. Maggie decided to tell her about the wolf. She stuffed her embroidery into the sleeve of her colorful feminine gown, "Dora, may I walk with you?"

Edita nodded her consent. "I'll be back," Maggie told Deborah, "I need to talk to Dora."

She stowed Dora's medicine bag by the ladies and walked through the market with her. Dora listened to Maggie's profuse, detailed account of killing the wolf.

"And Mama and Papa won't let me tell anyone. I can't even tell Deborah."

"Such things come out. See how excited you are. You're overflowing with this story. It's likely to spew out of you when you least expect it."

"Why can't I tell?"

"You can, of course. Your parents protect you by demanding discretion. Consider the consequences before you go against their wishes. They know what can happen. Do you?"

"Everyone could admire me."

"They could. Do you want that?"

"Yes, and Raamah could be jealous of me."

"Is that a good thing?"

"Yes, I like getting under his skin, but he can be mean."

"How could he be mean?"

"Oh, I don't know, but he always does something. He could tease me and say I'm unladylike."

"Who would believe him?"

"His sidekicks, his priest father, jealous men in the market, and vicious women at the well. Everyone except my loyal friends, I guess."

"Do those other people matter?"

"Not to me. I guess they matter to my parents."

"Why do they matter to your parents? Do those people have power over you?"

"Not really. I hardly know them."

"Could they influence your future?"

Maggie eyed a display of roasted nuts.

"I guess Mother's right about that." She blustered in exasperation. "It doesn't make sense to me. I don't understand why a man wouldn't want a wife who can defend herself."

"Men think they are supposed to defend their women and their wives should obey them. That's the custom. They're embarrassed if their wives show more prowess than they do. Women are expected to support their men and defer to them."

"Yes, I heard that in Leora's wedding ceremony. That's fine for her and Samuel because he nurtures her in return. He admires and appreciates her domestic skills, but most men take their women for granted. They think they're entitled to their attention and obedience."

"Enoch and Jonathan listen to Edita and Nanette."

"But Eban doesn't. I see how miserable Zadika is. I don't want that kind of relationship. I want to marry someone that I can support and admire. They must accept me as I am without trying to change me. They should admire and appreciate me like Samuel does Leora."

A peddler passed them pushing a cart of fresh vegetables.

"Maggie, why do you want people to know you killed a wolf?"

"It seems selfish to want them to admire me." She turned toward a display of fine cloth. "Maybe so everyone will know that part of what I am. Maybe I can be an example to other young people."

"If you want, you can let what other people think of you define you. Do you want to be put into the 'huntress' box?"

"I like that box. It makes me unique." She glanced down the street toward the market. "But I want to be more than that."

"Then do something spectacular with your other talents. How else do you want people to see you?"

"I want them to see me healing people with you."

Dora smiled her pleasure, "Thank you, Maggie. Is that all?"

"Kindness. I want to be kind."

Dora was pleased that Maggie's thoughts had changed to spiritual qualities. The conversation would be more productive now. "How will they know you are kind?"

"When they hear that I take care of people and animals, they'll know I'm reliable and trustworthy. Then they will ask me to help them."

A donkey with a load of skins ambled by. She caught up to price a wolf hide.

Returning to Dora, she said, "I want to attract a suitable mate. I think that's what Lizette does with her pretty dresses and flirty smiles. Leora has some of the same qualities, though she's always known Samuel was the one for her and made herself pleasing to him with her beauty and talent. Hopefully, Sarina will attract someone who appreciates her quietness and her skill at the loom."

"You have all those skills too."

"Yes, but I also tend sheep, kill wolves, and heal illnesses."

"Wonderful talents from a kind maiden! Except men want to kill the wolves."

"Yeah, but a wolf will steal a dozen lambs while Raamah gets scared and runs away."

Dora wondered why Maggie was preoccupied with Raamah.

"You weave and make pottery. Do you want people to know that you make beautiful things?"

"All the girls do those things."

"But not as good as you."

"True and no one's asking me to hide that."

They walked a few thoughtful, silent steps.

"Here's a good question for you. Why do you want anyone to be aware of you at all? Why should everyone know anything about you? I guess that if they know you killed a wolf by yourself, they'll think you're strong and courageous. What is there in you that wants a reputation? Why do you want attention?"

"It gives me eminence and importance."

"Is that something God wants with you?"

This gave Maggie pause. Dora pressed on.

"Does your own eminence further the light of God on earth?"

"No." She had to be honest. "No, it doesn't." She thought of the younger girls that she taught on the Sabbath. "It puts me between them and God. They think of me instead of God. If I'm overbearing, I block the flow of God's love."

"Strong personalities can do that. Maybe I'm doing that to you."

"Oh no! Not you, Dora. You're not like that at all. Raamah does that. So does Eban."

"Well some people, like Raamah, are jealous and deliberately spiteful. Eban is overbearing because of what he thinks he is supposed to do as priest. Even well-meaning souls can come between people and God. You must consciously invoke love and guidance if you want to mediate for God. You can't desire to expand your human personality."

"Don't I need a reputation? How will they know they can come to me for help? How will they know they can trust me?"

"God will guide them. You can't help everyone. You don't want a reputation greater than your ability to help. God will bring people for you to help. You don't have to do anything. Not everyone wants, needs, or is ready for the kind of help you can provide."

They rounded a corner where children played in the street.

"So do you think you'll tell the wolf story?" Dora asked.

"Not unless I'm asked. After all, I don't want to be a braggart who calls too much attention to herself. Killing the wolf was a good thing. It's perverse to act like it's bad. If I didn't kill it, someone else would need to. Otherwise, it would kill many lambs and injure shepherds. I did a service for the community."

They approached the well and Dora left Maggie with Edita, Sarina, and Deborah. She trusted Maggie to make her own decision. She was curious to see how it played out. She tried to think of boys that Maggie could support and admire. Maggie was superior to all of them to Dora's way of thinking. Raamah was accomplished, but mean. Dora thought he tormented Maggie because he had a crush on her. His taunts were designed to squash her so he could dominate her. It never worked. Dora imagined Maggie would live single before she would permit that.

Jesus was the only one that Dora thought Maggie could admire and support. If she married someone else, she would be settling. Jesus knew few other girls in Magdala, but she was sure that he had many admirers in Nazareth.

Maggie was about to find out how true this was.

When Maggie returned to the shade, Deborah told Edita and Sarina the latest news from Jonathan.

"Pa saw Joseph in Sepphoris. A rich merchant wants Jesus to marry his daughter."

Thoughts of the wolf flew from Maggie's mind.

Edita was surprised, "What merchant?"

"Ezra, from Nazareth."

Edita remembered him. He was a good man, a clever trader of textiles. "What's the daughter's name?"

"Rebecca. She's fallen in love with Jesus. She likes to watch him teach children at the synagogue. She thinks he will be a wonderful father." Deborah was proud of her cousin and couldn't help but brag, "He'll be a rabbi someday."

Sarina shook her head, "He can't do that until he marries."

"True, but he can when he marries Rebecca. She helps teach the children and wants to be a Rabbi's wife. She's beautiful and kind. It's a great match."

Deborah made a neat stitch in the scarf she was embellishing. "Rebecca told Miriam, Jesus' sister, how she felt about him. Then Miriam told her mother."

Edita was disturbed at the idea of Jesus marrying someone without Essene training. "What did Mary do?"

"She tried to discourage Rebecca. She and Miriam told her that Jesus had a special destiny to fulfill as a spiritual leader, that he wouldn't have time for home and family."

"That should turn away a merchant's spoiled and selfish daughter," Sarina said.

"You'd think so, but it made her more determined. She thinks he needs a faithful and efficient wife to share his career and she wants it to be her. Ezra will support them so Jesus can pursue his destiny without having to earn a living."

"Is Joseph arranging the marriage?" Edita asked thoughtfully.

"He's tempted. It would give Jesus a secure future, but he's letting Jesus decide. If he is truly chosen by God, he surely has the wisdom to decide."

Maggie imagined what Rebecca must be like. A merchant's daughter! She knew the type. She was beautiful. And pampered. She probably could never kill a wolf. She thinks she has leadership qualities. That won't help Jesus. She'll manipulate Jesus to go her way. She craves position and her father's wealth can buy it for herself and Jesus. She fancies herself gathering influence and controlling him.

Edita watched the reaction of her youngest daughter. Maggie was uncharacteristically silent, lost in thought on the subject of Jesus' marriage. She and Jesus had spent a lot of time together as children. She wondered what Maggie thought of him marrying Rebecca.

Edita grew more agitated with each step. The Brotherhood should have arranged his marriage before the birth. It was none of her own business who Jesus married or if he married at all, but she cared too much. She felt close to Mary because they studied and trained together at Mount Carmel. She had helped bring Jesus into the world and felt a special bond with him.

Once home, she went to Enoch in the shop and closed the door. "How could Joseph and Mary let this happen?"

Enoch looked up from painting, "Joseph and Mary?" He needed to keep working. This wasn't a normal day. With so many diversions, he would work overtime on his orders.

"So you don't know. I guess you haven't seen Jonathan. A merchant is marrying his daughter to Jesus."

Enoch stopped his brush mid-air, forgot about the design he was crafting, and asked, "How do you know?"

"Deborah told us at the well. Jonathan saw Joseph in Sepphoris and they talked to Ezra in the market."

"It's hard to believe Jesus is ready for that, but he is at the age of responsibility. He's pleasant, good looking, and smart. Of course young ladies are attracted to him." Enoch wiped his brush and put it in a cup of water.

"Jesus needs to marry someone who can help establish the kingdom of God on earth. Can a merchant's daughter, trained only in the strict Jewish tradition do that?" Edita paced the floor near the potter's wheel. "Does she know spiritual principles? Can she invoke the light of God and feel the pressure of the silence?"

Enoch introduced reason to her thinking, "We don't know that she can't."

"You know what priests teach. Can she initiate the new vibration of forgiveness and peace or is she entrenched in the 'eye for an eye' mentality of retaliation. Does she still believe Jews are God's chosen people that he sends to kill and be killed? Does she see the futility of law and punishment?"

Enoch scraped dried clay off the wheel while Edita continued her rant.

Edita believed a merchant's daughter would be attached to the things of earth. "Can she understand the concept of limitlessness? Can she vision eternal infinity beyond time and form?"

Edita picked up the broom and swept like she was killing snakes, "She will take worldly possessions for granted. How can she possibly know about communing with the intelligences within the earth, water, wind, and fire and feel close to nature. Her father is trying to buy Jesus for her. She's materialistic."

Edita swept the shavings around Enoch's stool, "Seed ideas need to be established for spiritual community in the incoming age."

She moved the stool to access a pile of shavings. "Do you think this Rebecca has ever conversed with God? Can she conceive of herself as a sun of light in oneness with all or visualize a crown of the light of truth across her forehead and a mantle of honor surrounding her. Will she hear the music of the spheres, see the celestial radiance, feel divine love, or smell the sweet fragrance of elemental life? Will she understand the light of Christ in all?"

She swept a pile of shavings into a pan. Enoch tried to console her. "It's strange to us, but we don't know exactly how things should happen. God gave us free will. He did the same for Jesus, and Rebecca."

"Free will, my foot! We pledged to bring in the next dispensation according to guidance. Jesus should marry someone in touch with spirit."

Enoch sensed that Edita was out of arguments. He sighed, "We don't know anything about Rebecca. She could have training we don't know about like Maggie gets from Dora. The girl can learn what she needs to know from Jesus, Mary, and Joseph."

Edita leaned on the broom, "What if she refuses to learn?"

She tackled a stubborn dollop of clay on the floor then answered her own question. "But I guess she won't refuse since she fancies herself in love with Jesus. Jewish daughters learn to obey their husbands."

Enoch hid an unbelieving smirk while he scraped the hardened deposit of clay. He didn't believe Edita ever obeyed him.

She groaned, "Look at Zadika. She's frustrated trying to please Eban."

She paused pensively, "I suppose Rebecca will happily obey Jesus. He will be a great spiritual teacher."

Enoch thought that line of thinking showed promise, "True. She'll obey Jesus and all will be well."

Edita shook her head. The hard clay was loose now and she made powerful strokes with the broom. "Obeying is for the birds." She paused to address him emphatically. "If both partners are in tune with their guidance and follow it, there is no need for any ordering and obeying."

Enoch couldn't argue with that. He avoided giving Edita orders. He wondered what it would be like for his wife to obey him, but hoped he would never find out. He smiled at the thought. He was glad she trusted him and shared her concerns. He thought he wouldn't like an obedient wife. How boring and lonely that would be!

"Have you talked to Nanette about this?"

"No, and I won't." She paused, spied the dust pan in the corner, and brought it to her pile of debris.

"Maybe I will if she brings it up. She is Mary's sister-in-law and I won't tell her how I feel about this. Our friendship is too precious to me."

"What did you think would happen when Jesus reached marriageable age?" Enoch asked.

She swept the waste into the pan. "I thought that he would stay single or choose someone from the White Brotherhood."

"Young ladies can learn the Essene ways without going to Mount Carmel or being born into an Essene family."

"But it should be ingrained. Otherwise, they'll revert to old ways when things get tough."

She dumped the content of the pan into a waste can and looked around the room. "Looks like we got you all cleaned up." She propped the broom against the wall. "See you at supper." She left the door open on her way to the house.

Is he going to marry Rebecca?

Not according to our curriculum. Is this part of the plan to keep him away from the Magdalene?

It's an idea.

Aren't you afraid it might work? Our suns need to unite eventually. His marriage would end that.

How else can we keep them apart?

Go back to the original idea. Put distance between them.

We have no control from this side. When they crossed the veil into Maya, they became subject to free will. Jesus can do whatever suits his ego.

Suppose he marries Rebecca. Can our curriculums still work?

Yes they can. Our suns can still balance electromagnetic energy for the planet without consummating it in the earthly illusion.

No, they can't! . . . . Well, I guess they can, but it'll be too weak to be fruitful through the generations. It's mighty, dynamic, and more intense if manifested through embodied beings.

We must be patient. Wait for Jesus to make his choice.

CHAPTER 9

Later that evening, Maggie found Edita shelling beans on the patio. She filled a basin with legumes.

"Mom, what did Deborah mean when she said Jesus was chosen by God?

"We're all chosen by God, dear, just for different things."

"Then why mention it? Is Jesus chosen for something special?"

Edita had to think about this. Was being the mother of the messiah more important than being a whole woman, an Essene maiden more special than a merchant's daughter, a messiah more blessed than a rabbi, a potter, or fisherman?

She picked up a bowl, "Every person is important to the whole just like each stroke is important to designs on your father's pottery. But there is a central part to each design that gets more attention."

"Like the largest flower surrounded by others."

"Yes, all the other flowers and vines are important to the design like we are all necessary for God's plan. We complete him."

Maggie snapped the end of a pod and pulled the string down its side. "Is Jesus the big flower in the center?"

Edita hesitated, wondering what her answer would mean to Maggie. "Some of the Essene Brotherhood believe he was born to be the messiah."

Maggie was shocked. To her, Jesus was just a good friend. "You mean I use to play with the messiah?"

Edita nodded and put more beans in her pan.

Maggie remembered the unusual things she saw with Jesus: Playing with the undines in the Sea of Galilee, talking to a gnome, healing Zadika. He made rare things seem ordinary and common things effortless. In her childhood innocence she found them normal, not remarkable. She hadn't even told anyone about them.

Now, more mature after time away from Jesus, she saw how extraordinary they were. Of course, there was that time he weeded Dora's garden. Dora saw his potential and knew he could heal Zadika.

Realization flowed into Maggie. If Jesus was the messiah, he would be king. He would raise an army to drive the Romans out of Israel.

"Does Rebecca know he's the messiah?"

"Evidently not."

"So she's going to marry him thinking he's a rabbi and become queen when he's king."

"That's the way it seems. Priests tell us the messiah will save God's people. We Essenes believe there is a deeper spiritual purpose for the messiah. He will teach us that we are divine children of God."

Maggie thought that a grand thing. Rebecca would be the wife of a wise and gracious king. Queen of the Jews. A merchant's daughter born into privilege would know how to be queen. She would give orders to servants, wear fine clothes, and socialize with royalty from other lands.

Perhaps Rebecca was right for Jesus. Maggie grieved over the loss of her friend. Once he was married, it would be improper for him to have a close female friend.

Maggie wondered what life might be like for a messiah. She knew Israel expected a man to come, become King, and save them from the Romans. The idea of Jesus being such a man mystified her. He was nice, but not kingly.

She hungrily reread the Bible to recall what the prophets said about a messiah. She found the passages unsatisfactory, too vague to understand. Something about a 'star' from Jacob, ruling Israel, smiting enemies, and destroying cities. That didn't sound like something Jesus would do.

Another predicted there would be a prophet that would be a spokesman to the people. He might do that.

A king of God's choice would be enthroned in Jerusalem and given all the nations in the world if he only asked. Why would Jesus want nations?

In Psalm 110, the Lord said to the messiah, 'Rule as my regent. I will subdue your enemies and make them bow down low before you.'

Maggie supposed Jesus could change to be like that when he got older.

She wondered what Psalm 21 meant when it said something about a crown and throne of fame, honor, splendor, majesty, happiness, and joy. That didn't sound like something you could sit on.

Isaiah described a messiah as king, ruler of David's house, who would come to restore and reform the Jewish nation and purify the church. She liked the part that said the blessings of restoration would be shared by gentiles. She and Jesus agreed on that.

Micah said Bethlehem would be the birthplace of God's King, that he would 'feed' his 'flock,' and be honored around the world. He will be our peace. ~If that's true, then the part in Numbers about him destroying many cities couldn't be true. ~

Then Israel will refresh the world, be strong as a lion, and God will destroy all the weapons. ~So which will it be, war or peace?~ she wondered.

Maggie was horrified by the dire predictions in Zechariah that he will be pierced and mourned, that all of Israel will weep. Then a fountain would open to cleanse them from sins and wickedness. That part sounded promising.

Maggie had heard those passages in the synagogue, had read them with Edita and Sarina in her lessons. But then they were detached ideas about events generations away, not something that would happen soon, and certainly not involving anyone she knew. Now, she considered the implications as if they were all about Jesus.

She supposed even a well-loved king, chosen by God, would have enemies. David even had enemies. And some of them might kill him. She didn't want Jesus to suffer such a fate.

She was alternately glad and terrified. Glad Jesus was loved and anointed by God, but terrified of his violent death.

Gone were her dreams of a peaceful, pastoral life with Jesus as a friend. His friends would be wealthy, highly placed. His servants would come from the lower class. His betrothed was a wealthy merchant's daughter. She felt the distance widen between them.

Maggie knew his life would not include her. He would grow older, marry, and take his position as a rabbi. She supposed a prophet would anoint him like Samuel did David. Then he would distinguish himself in battle and take the throne.

She couldn't picture herself in that kind of scenario. She went about her business tending sheep, teaching young girls on the Sabbath, and helping Dora on her healing calls. She supposed some young man would eventually ask her father for her hand.

Maggie ground herbs at Dora's with a mortar and pestle, "Dora, what do you think about the messiah?"

"I've heard talk about it for years. Different people say different things. They can't all be true."

"You bet they're not. I've been reading about it, but there's not much about it in the Bible. What's there doesn't agree. Some say he'll be a king, others a prophet. He'll fight and destroy, he'll bring peace. He'll purify and restore the Jewish nation, he'll save the gentiles."

It amused Dora that Maggie found contradictions about the messiah. She sensed Maggie had more than a passing interest in the subject. "Even so, people speculate about it all the time. People who are oppressed need something to give them hope. Expecting a messiah does that for them. Do you want to believe in a messiah, Maggie?"

"I don't know. I guess so. Not if he brings war though. War brings death, grief, rape, and pillage. I don't want that. I don't want Dan and Samuel to steal spoils of war. The commandments outlaw killing, adultery, and stealing."

"If you think Dan and Samuel will be involved, then you think the messiah is coming soon."

"Well, not real soon. No one's training our boys to be soldiers yet. Can't we leave well enough alone? The Romans don't bother us too much. We have a good way of life."

"Things happen for a reason." Dora poured the ground herbs on the table. "Why are you suddenly interested in the messiah? What have you heard?"

"Mother said Jesus might be the messiah."

~Ah,~ Dora thought, ~Just as I expected.~ "No wonder you're concerned. He's a good friend to you."

"It doesn't make sense to me. I can't imagine Jesus destroying cities and being king."

Dora took a flat knife and channeled herb dust into a flask. "What if he's a peaceful prophet? That would make more sense."

"But the worst part is that he'll be despised and rejected, pierced and mourned. Such tragedy! Why tragedy?"

"Many great men have died tragic deaths. David. Samson."

"If they're anointed by God, they should have happier endings."

"I think that depends on what they are anointed to do."

"I don't even know why I'm concerned. I'll be here herding, teaching, and healing. I'll never see Jesus again. He's in Nazareth with Rebecca."

"Wait a minute. Rebecca?"

"That's Jesus' betrothed, the one he's marrying."

"Oh, of course." Dora continued grinding. ~So that's it. Is this a change in destiny or a glitch along the way? Even children of promise have lessons to learn. Jesus can marry in his youth like most Jewish boys, enter a profession, and have a family.~ Dora was vaguely disappointed that he might take such a pedestrian, unremarkable path. ~Maybe he's not the messiah. Edita and I could be wrong. Maggie's concern could be pointless. ~

Maggie watched the boys enviously as they passed the well and went straight to the synagogue for schooling, unlike the girls who stopped at the well to get water for their homes, "Sarina, do you wonder what it's like to go to school?"

"I don't know. I guess it's like our lessons at home except with all boys from different families."

"They have a real teacher and we only have Mama and Papa."

"Mama and Papa are teachers. They taught us."

"It's not the same. The boys have a rabbi with synagogue training."

"I don't guess they learn anything we don't. They learn to read and study the Bible."

"I guess they discuss it too."

"So did we."

"But the rabbi explains what it means."

"Mama and Papa explained."

"Yes, but Mama and Papa aren't traditional."

"I wonder how different they are."

"I don't know. Dan knows. We can ask him."

Dan came around the bend with the sheep. Maggie accosted him. "Dan, what do boys do in the synagogue school?"

"They learn to read Hebrew and write Aramaic. They learn the history of Israel, the feasts of commemoration, the Sabbath rites."

"What did you read?"

"We read the Book of the Law in Hebrew and memorized the sacred laws."

"Why memorize them?"

"We only have one text, so we have to keep information in our heads."

"How do you do that?"

"We take turns reading while others repeat aloud what is read. We studied Leviticus, the Prophets, and the Psalms. Scriptures in Hebrew. After our Bar Mitzvahs, we are allowed to read scriptures in the Sabbath service, except when prominent visitors come to do it."

"How did you first start to read and write?"

"At first, we sat in a semicircle on the floor facing the rabbi and took turns reciting while others wrote in the sand."

"How is that different from what we learned from Mama and Papa?"

"We didn't learn Greek in synagogue school."

"Why not?"

"It's considered secular and evil because Greeks don't believe in the one God."

"But we have to communicate with Roman soldiers. They speak Greek."

"That's the reason we are fortunate. In our family, Mama and Papa teach us Greek. We learned Sanskrit at home, but not in the synagogue. Rabbis think it's not important because there are no Jewish writings in Sanskrit.

"We learned Bible stories and the law from Mama and Papa, but they have an expanded view of life that goes beyond what is written. The rabbi teaches what he was taught: the law and its enforcements and punishments. Mama and Papa's way of life expands beyond that. They do not worry about the law. They live natural goodness without guilt or need to defend.

"Some priests are obsessed with doing what the law says and forget why the law was made in the first place. Mama and Papa never forget love, caring and sharing, giving and receiving. They apply spiritual principles to everyday life. They are very practical."

Sarina shifted her water skin to her other shoulder. "Don't the rabbis, priests, and chazzans[1] also do that?"

"Some more than others," Dan admitted. "But they are judged by the public eye. They make a big show of following the law so no one can condemn them. What do you think of the priest?"

Maggie and Sarina knew what they thought. "Eban? He's stern and proper."

"And boring."

"He thinks that's what he's supposed to be. He doesn't rest and enjoy life like Mama and Papa. He probably doesn't even relax with his family."

Maggie cringed distastefully, feeling sorry for Raamah in spite of herself. "I don't think I would want a priest for a father. I wouldn't want to be one either."

"But Mama and Papa take pleasure in walking with God. They do everything mindfully, letting the love of God flow through them. They make inspiration and guidance practical in everything they do."

Sarina nodded reflectively, "That's true isn't it? Mama, especially with her cooking."

Maggie agreed, "And Papa with his pottery. They both do things exquisitely."

Dan knew his sisters understood, "Yes. That's how they care, share, and extend the love of God."

Maggie was awed, "We've done this all our lives. I didn't know."

"That's what you do when you weave, Sarina," Dan said.

"And what you do too, Maggie," Sarina said, "with stickball, Dora's healing, and singing and playing your harp."

"Leora with dancing and Batia with embroidery," Maggie added.

"Samuel and Jonathan with fishing."

"Nanette with gardening."

"And Dan, you with being a loving brother and son," Maggie said.

"About that . . ."

"What Dan?"

"I want to be a chazzan."

---

[1] cantor or person who leads songful prayer.

"That's exciting," Sarina said. "You'll be wonderful. You will teach the rituals, be cantor, and teach songs. You've taught us all our lives."

Maggie clasped her hands in gladness. "Yes, you have. Living with you and Leora, and Mama and Papa was like having two sets of parents when we were young."

"And you taught us. You knew we could learn even though we are girls."

"Do Mama and Papa know you want to be a chazzan?"

"I'm reluctant to tell Papa because he still needs my help with the sheep and the shop."

"That's silly, Dan," Maggie said. "You should do what you're guided to do. You're inspired. Look at how you explained Mama and Papa's ways to us. You are a wonderful teacher. I'll help Papa with the sheep."

"And I'll help him in the shop," Sarina said, "Mama and Papa will be thrilled."

As far as they were concerned, the matter was settled.

"Let's tell them at supper tonight," Maggie suggested.

"The two of you can't act like you know. They have to think they were first to know, except for Batia, of course."

"We'll get Samuel and Leora to come."

Sarina reassured him, "It'll be great, Dan. We'll arrange it."

"Okay. I'll invite Samuel when I see him today. You make sure Leora knows in time."

"Maggie, let's prepare dessert over at Leora's. That way, Mama won't know something special is about to happen."

Dan warned them again, "Remember you can't act like you know. They'll know something's up if you make a fuss."

Sarina waved him off, "Not if Leora and Samuel just happen to drop in with a cake. We won't have to worry about the rest. Mama's food is always special and there's always more than enough. We don't even have to clean house. Her house is always clean."

"Immaculate," Dan agreed.

The evening went as expected. Enoch and Edita were happy with Dan's future as chazzan and gratified that this would give Dan a way to slip some Essene truth to the boys of Magdala. He and Samuel definitely had a broader knowledge base than other young men.

"Sarina, we could teach the girls."

"No, we can't. We are not rabbis or chazzans."

"We know what they need to learn and we're good with children. Mothers trust us. They bring the little ones to us to baby sit."

"We'll get in trouble. Girls are not allowed to learn what boys know."

Maggie expected Sarina to recite every reason why they could not start a girl's school.

"We already take care of their basic needs and play with them. What's wrong with teaching them a few letters and words?"

Sarina admitted it would be easy to do a little more.

"They bring their children to us when they go to the market or get together to sew or preserve food."

"But we don't see them often enough to teach them much."

"So we see them more. Most mothers would love for their daughters to read and write."

"They'll be afraid to."

"Who'll know then? If they're afraid, they won't tell."

"Maggie," Sarina chided doubtfully.

"We can teach them to weave, embroider, and cook. That way, we'll have something to tell them if anyone asks. We'll call it a girls' club."

Sarina looked thoughtful.

Maggie knew she was getting interested, "I think I could get Deborah, Janette, and Lizette to help us."

"Lizette? What does she know?"

"She's great at grooming and dress. She embroiders well and is tactful and diplomatic."

"All right. I guess they can't spend all of their time reading and weaving. Are you going to teach them how to herd and heal?"

Maggie grinned. She knew she had Sarina now. "It wouldn't hurt to teach them simple first aid and how to care for animals. We'll make a schedule."

"You could have a girls' stickball team."

"We need enough girls for two teams so they can play games."

"I was only kidding," Sarina said cautiously.

"Are you going to ask Janette to help?" Maggie asked.

"Of course. Deborah and Janette are as qualified as we are. They learned to read like we did. Remember the times we went over to learn from Nanette and when they came to our house to learn from Mama?"

Edita knew something was brewing when Maggie and Sarina sat down at the kitchen table while she kneaded. She gave the dough a hearty punch in the middle, "What's up?"

Maggie spoke, "We have an idea and we want your help."

Edita was always ready to help her girls, "What's your idea?"

"We would like to turn our baby sitting into a girls' club."

"I've never heard of a girls' club. Girls and women have gathered together since the beginning of time. They never called it a club." She pushed the dough with the heels of her hands. "Why have a club?"

"To teach girls life skills," Sarina explained.

"Such as...?" Edita folded the dough.

"Cooking, gardening, reading, music, weaving, embroidery, writing . . ."

Flour scattered on Evita's dark tunic when she put her hands on her hips, "Stop right there. You want to teach girls to read and write?"

"That would be part of it," Maggie defended, "but they will also learn other feminine arts."

"That way," Sarina said logically, "if anyone asks what we teach, we can tell them something without mentioning reading and writing."

Edita absently wiped her hands on her frock, "Oh, I see. You want to teach them to read and write and you're including the other things as a smoke screen."

"It'll work," Maggie said persuasively. "People don't believe girls are smart enough to read and write. If we said we were teaching them, no one would believe us."

Edita shaped the dough into a ball, "Where are you going to have this school?"

"Not school, Mother," Maggie corrected, "Girls' club."

"Yeah right," Edita pinched the dough into balls.

Sarina continued, "We could teach on the plaza by the synagogue."

Edita placed the rolls on a baking slab, "I don't think you can have your reading and writing lessons there. It's a good place for singing, storytelling, and embroidery. You need privacy for writing and reading."

Maggie asked for what they really wanted, "Can we have it here, Mama?"

Edita placed the rolls in the oven, "This is big. We'll have to talk to your father." She slid the oven door shut.

At the supper table, Enoch listened patiently to Maggie and Sarina's idea for the girls' club. He looked at his bright daughters, so young, but already marriageable age. They were past the age of responsibility and he was proud of their accomplishments. Now they showed that they were not only smart and talented, also altruistic. They had learned things other girls did not and they wanted to share. Could he say no?

Edita had prepared him for the girls' proposal and, together, they decided what to do. He listened intently with his elbows on the table, his hands clasped in front of his chin until they told him everything. This was a risk to their status in the community, but he and Edita were sworn to advance education on earth and this way was a great way to do it.

"You need an adult present. Though you have all had your bat mitzvah, you need someone who is older and more experienced."

Maggie and Sarina looked at Edita imploringly.

She took their hint, "Not just me. I'm willing to take my turn, but I'll do it once a week."

"Okay," Maggie improvised, "Let's ask Nanette, Leora, Batia, and Dora to be our sponsors with you."

Enoch nodded approvingly, "Let me know when they've agreed. You have to prepare materials every day and clean up afterward."

Sarina and Maggie quickly agreed.

"When you teach reading and writing, have them write sentences from stories, copy the law, copy recipes, and make domestic schedules and instructions. Don't give them the idea that you're teaching them to read and write, but helping them to remember what they learn. I don't want to be summoned before the elders for giving women ideas. They think women should stay in their place. We don't want to cross the line, just nudge it over."

In their excitement, Sarina and Maggie struggled to keep still.

Enoch was all business. "Think about how you're going to recruit girls to join the club. How long will the meetings be? Who will teach what? What procedures will be used? What materials do you need? Make a list of everything you think they need to learn. Make it practical. Don't overextend yourselves or try to teach too much too soon. Teach a little at a time, but teach it thoroughly. Learning builds upon itself. There are things they have to learn before they can learn others. Those are prerequisite skills and concepts called basics. Start with those. Until you get a good start, you have to tell me your plans for each day at supper the night before.

"Children are perceptive and smart. They can learn as much as adults. You make it psychologically attractive for them by assuming their level of whimsy and play.

"Teach because you enjoy learning. Teaching teaches you that you have learned. You will never be more certain of anything than you are after you teach it. Sharing anything expands and multiplies it whether it is thoughts, feelings, or things. Whatever you share not only stays with you, but also returns to you."

Sarina and Maggie were busy the next day. Sarina was fun to work with. She was smart with great ideas and Maggie trusted her like no one else. Sarina was her sister and was always in her life. They visited Dora to share their ideas and get her promise to help. She invited them to meet the club at her place periodically to assist in the preparation of herbs and oils. They went to Nanette's to get her agreement to be a chaperone. She asked them to meet in her garden on occasion. Leora agreed to participate and teach folk dances. Batia would assist with embroidery. Deborah and Janette agreed to be counselors and part of the teaching team.

The four counselors gathered to plan. They were a team and their similar backgrounds enabled them to agree quickly. They decided to do crafts, music, storytelling, and gardening together. Each one would take charge of their strongest area of interest and the others would assist. During each activity, they would teach words for each lesson. Then they would meet in a semicircle to trace words in the sand in the privacy of Enoch's courtyard enclosed by the house, barn, garden, and shop. The young girls would bring supplies from their homes and keep their completed projects or give them as gifts.

They discussed how to attract girls for the club. Deborah proposed they sit by the well with headbands for the girls. "That will attract them to us and we can give them a headband when we invite them to come to our first club meeting." Janette suggested distributing headbands in the market, or giving them to mothers to give to their girls. Sarina suggested that Maggie take them with her when she went on calls with Dora.

Maggie nodded her agreement, "We could visit girls who we know would benefit from a girls' club.

"I want to ask Lizette to help us."

"She can't read."

"No, she can't, but she's good with children, with fashion and beauty, and with domestic arts. She's not as flighty as she seems. She's competent and reliable. She'll appeal to girls because they admire her. She can help us get the word out."

The others grudgingly considered it. Janette suggested they invite her to help them make the headbands. "Then we could see how we feel about it afterward."

Maggie was delighted, "Good, she might even learn to read while teaching the girls. She has a great personality and a caring and sharing attitude. Believe me. You'll like her."

They gathered to make headbands of thread that Sarina and Janette spun from wool dyed purple, red, blue, and yellow. They left the fleece loose around the floss and combed it into a fluffy texture as they wove the bands. They were imaginative statements of creativity.

Lizette wove as well as they did. She exuded enthusiasm for the primary colors and the flashy design, "These are unique. What girl wouldn't love to have one of these? Let's advertise by wearing them everywhere for a couple of weeks. I'll carry extra ones in my sleeve pocket when I go to the market so I can give them to girls I see."

Sarina ran colorful fiber across the warp. "Lizette, would you like to sit at the well with us for a couple of days?"

"What fun! We can take our little looms with us and make more headbands. And some of us can embroider."

Janette separated a thread from the hank, "Good, that way, the girls will know we are going to do things and they'll want to be with us."

"Let's take some of Mama's sweet rolls," Maggie said while she twisted the loose end of her skein.

Deborah pulled a woof thread evenly across the width of the headband she was working on. "I'll bring some apples from Ma's orchard."

"Maggie, could you bring a vial of scented oil from Dora?" Sarina said while she neatly tucked the end threads into the fabric she made. "Okay, this is great. All the girls in Magdala will look and smell the same. We'll establish a presence they'll want to be a part of."

Sarina held up her headband for all to see, "Oh yes. We need to get Mother and Nanette to talk about it at the next women's gathering."

In a few days, they saw girls wearing colorful headbands everywhere they went. Anticipation for the girls' club was building.

CHAPTER 10

Girls came from every walk of life: daughters of craftsmen, fishermen, merchants, shepherds, rabbis, farmers, slaves, and servants. The counselors were delighted. They loved to think they were blurring class lines.

Maggie started the meeting with a simple song accompanying herself on the harp. The girls quickly joined the song. The counselors introduced themselves and talked about the purpose of the club. They would care and share and help each other, learn new things and ideas, and meet in various places depending on what they were going to do.

They walked to the shore of the Sea of Galilee and sat on an outcropping of rock while Janette told a story. Sarina led them along the shore to pick up smooth or colorful rocks. Deborah removed her sandals and walked into the sea followed by giggling girls. While their feet dried, they sat in a circle in the damp sand and used sticks to draw the letters in the word 'water.' They sang a song of gratitude to God and water, and then put on their sandals before returning to Enoch's. The girls felt comfortable and friendly. They ran to catch up and hold the counselors' hands on the way back. They promised to make whatnots of their rocks the next day.

The counselors were pleased with their first 'get acquainted' meeting. The girls had been a little timid and quiet. That evening, Enoch told them not to worry about the initial shyness. It was expected the first day. "They'll get comfortable with you and each other in a few days. Then their personalities will come out. Show them you care about them. Give them individual attention during activities and ask them about their families and what they like and dislike. Find something they like that you like and tell them something similar about yourself. It won't be long before they talk all the time."

Maggie sat under an olive tree in the plaza across from the synagogue with her harp, surrounded by young girls of Magdala. She thought that Jesus and Rebecca were doing the same thing in Nazareth. The girls sat at Maggie's feet, enraptured by her tale of Deborah, the prophetess. They were angry at King Jabin for terrorizing Israel with his nine hundred iron chariots, awed that Deborah held court under a palm tree, hopeful when she summoned Barak, and gratified when he gathered ten thousand men from Naphtali and Zebulum. They were confident there would be victory because the Lord had told Deborah what to do. They were excited when Deborah and Barak's army came down Mt. Tabor and chased Sisera's men down the Kishon River, joyful that the Lord stirred the enemy into a panic, disappointed when Commander Sisera escaped, breathless when Jael hid him and gave him milk, and cheered lustily when she drove the tent peg through Sisera's head into the ground. They were gratified when Israel became strong and King Jabin weaker until he and all his people were destroyed and there was peace in the land for forty years.

After the tale, Maggie sang the ballad of Deborah and Barak's victory and Sisera's death at the hand of Jael.

Maggie chose this story because it illustrated two strong women in action. She wanted them to learn that women are not helpless. She listened idly to their banter as she put away her harp.

"Why did Barak want Deborah to go with him into battle?"

"Because he was afraid."

"Maybe the men didn't trust him enough to lead them."

"Why did she call Barak? Why didn't she just do it herself?"

"Maybe she needed his military expertise."

"What if she had stayed home?"

"Then Barak would have gotten all the credit."

"This way he had to share it with women."

"Yeah, he had to share it with Deborah and Jael."

"Yes, Jael killed the leader of the enemy. Sisera was a coward to leave his men."

"Jael must have been scared when a strange man came to her tent."

"Yes, his clothes were probably torn."

"And he stank of blood and sweat."

"She was brave and smart. Instead of running away, she made him trust her by hiding and feeding him. Then she waited for him to fall asleep before she did him in."

"A man couldn't have done that."

"A man would have had to challenge him to a duel. Men can't slay another man if they're not looking."

"But women can because we're not strong enough to fight men and we don't know how to use weapons."

"If we're frightened, we have to be crafty."

"Men shouldn't frighten us."

"They think we can't defend ourselves because we're weak, but we can because we're smarter."

Maggie was amused at the girls' reactions to the story of Deborah and Jael. She supposed it was as good to defend yourself by fighting battles and killing men as it was to manipulate a man into marrying you as Ruth and Naomi did in another Bible story. Both showed that women had options and could get their way. She plaintively thought of Rebecca's manipulations of Jesus.

Out of the corner of her eye, Maggie saw Raamah half hidden by another tree in the plaza. He waited thoughtfully while the girls joined their mothers. Maggie busily adjusted her harp strap as he walked toward her. She had seen his devotion to Zadika and thought she should trust him more, but she remembered his ridicule too vividly. She put on a welcoming smile.

He walked by her on her way home. She was uncomfortable, but since he walked beside her, she thought she should talk to him. She waited for him to make derisive remarks while trying to think how to start a conversation. Ah. She knew one thing she could ask him. "How's your Mother?"

"She's in wonderful health. That poultice that the Nazarene brought worked wonders for her."

"Dora's a gifted healer." Maggie was wary of this topic. She was sure he was looking for sarcastic ways to mock her. Also, she didn't want him to know it was actually Jesus who had healed his mother.

"That's the only time I've seen her work," he said. "The people I know come to the Temple for healing."

She was more comfortable with this line of conversation, "Zadika is wonderful to visit the poor, widows, and orphans."

He agreed, "I went with her on her rounds when I was a boy."

Maggie thought it strange that he would use past tense, but it was appropriate. He was no longer a boy, she no longer a mere girl. They both were of age having been through their mitzvah.

"When did you stop going with her?"

"When I entered the synagogue school. I didn't want other boys to make fun of me for doing women's work. I was too busy then anyway."

"I suppose you were too young to help when you went with her."

"I carried supplies."

They walked wordlessly along the street for a while.

"You sang Deborah's victory song beautifully."

She was stunned. Raamah had never complimented her before. She didn't know what to say. She looked at him with a question in her eyes. "You don't mean that."

"Yes, I do." He wasn't pleased that she made him nervous. "I assure you, I do."

"You're not going to make a sarcastic remark?"

"No."

"You're not going to say that I sing like a girl."

"No. You do, of course, but that's a good thing."

"You're not going to ask me how I, a woman, know a song of battle."

"I suppose your father taught you."

She didn't divulge that her mother had taught her. Then he would know that the women in her family read. She decided to let it go at that. He might turn anything she said or did into something to use against her.

"You're not going to say that I'm showing off?"

"No, are you?"

"No, I'm merely sharing with young girls. You're not going to say I have no business telling stories by the synagogue?"

"No, who better?"

She had to agree that no one could do it better than she.

"You really care about those girls. You have a real gift."

"They are a challenge. They each have a mind of their own."

"How you marshal them to listen to a story is beyond me, but you do it effortlessly. It's magical."

"They inspire me. That expression on their faces when they're waiting with bated breath to hear what I'm going to say next makes me want to make them even more excited."

Raamah felt the warmth of Maggie's open smile.

She stopped in front of her house and looked at him suspiciously, "What are you up to, Raamah?"

He shrugged off the question, "Nothing."

She didn't believe him. "This is my house."

"I know."

"Why did you follow me home?"

"Just to talk."

"What do we need to talk about?"

"Nothing."

She was exasperated, "I'm going inside."

"Okay."

She dismissed him, "Bye."

A lone runner came up the path to Dora's hut. "It's Ebelina. It's her time." Dora and Maggie made haste with the messenger carrying the birthing bag. It held a knife, string, reeds for suction to clear babies' noses and mouths; containers of cumin, hyssop, and mint oil; and soft baby blankets. Maggie had started going to births with Dora after her mitzvah.

When they entered the home, an agonized wail greeted them from the inner room where they found Ebelina on soft, clean sheets; exhausted from pain and terrified of the next contraction. Ebelina's mother, Ella, had done all she could and sent for Dora when she realized that her knowledge gained from having her own children was not enough.

Dora comforted Ebelina and her plaintive cries subdued. She scrubbed her hands and arms and held them up to avoid touching anything unclean. She felt Ebelina's belly to determine the child's position while Maggie discarded and replenished the water.

Ebelina breathed faster and harder, confident now that Dora was there. She emitted guttural sounds, gathering strength for the next onslaught. Dora recognized it as a mother's final preparation for birth. The next pain came, excruciating to the extreme. As it subsided, Dora asked Maggie to count until the next contraction so they would know how far apart the pains were.

Maggie concentrated on counting while Dora set everyone at ease with tales of other successful births, talk of recent weddings, and accounts of local events.

Dora checked to be sure Ebelina was comfortable. She directed Ella to hold her daughter's hand for moral support. Maggie organized the herbal remedies.

Dora instructed Ebelina to squat next to the bed with the next contraction and got in position to catch the baby. After three more contractions, the baby's head appeared and retreated back in the womb before the last pain waned.

"Take a breath and get ready to push next time," Dora said.

One more contraction brought the baby's head out further. "Breathe," said Dora, "Now. Push."

The baby emerged into Dora's welcoming arms. They helped Ebelina back to bed and laid the baby near her breast. The baby gulped, gave a lusty cry, and latched on. Dora cut the cord and Maggie rubbed the baby with a warm towel. It wasn't long before she laid the baby on warm blankets and cleared its nose and mouth with a piece of cloth. She helped Ebelina get comfortable while Dora wrapped the baby snuggly and laid her beside her mother. The mother began nursing her child that she called Evita, life.

This was one of the happier births Maggie attended with Dora. Most mothers were more vocal when expressing their pain. Some babies came too fast, some feet first, some were stillborn. She watched Dora resuscitate babies who were not breathing when they came out of the womb and sighed in sorrow when a mother died and Dora cut open her womb to save the child.

Fathers reacted differently. Most were happy to be fathers. Some were disappointed if the child was a girl. One swooned when his wife died in childbirth. Another took a healthy child and sold it into slavery. One put a deformed child out to die. Life could be brutal.

Families gave Dora gifts of gratitude in payment for her services. Foodstuffs came in the form of grain or flour, fruit and vegetables, oil or wine, or seeds for her garden. Her patients gave her bolts of linen or wool, fiber or skeins of thread. They presented trinkets: brass and copper bangles, crafted jewelry, and hair combs.

Dora had a diverse assortment of animals in her barnyard due to the preferences of her clients. Some gave her solid yearling goats, others spotted ones. Some offered speckled hens, others white, brown, or red. The motley animals lived in her compound harmoniously; glad to be tokens of gratitude and willing to serve her. She accepted all with grace and cheer, happily surrounded in the quaintness that this variety afforded her.

Maggie was grateful to Dora for introducing her to ways of thinking that were outside the rigidity of the Jewish tradition. Her childish talks with Jesus had opened her mind and heart even further. She was schooled in compassion by helping Dora tend to ailments in Magdala. Where other girls would be nauseous at the horrific sights of gross sores, body secretions, and vomit, Maggie observed them dispassionately for the information they gave about the person's illness and did what needed to be done. Instead of being repulsed by the deaf, blind, and aged, Maggie felt a positive connection with them. Their capacity for gratitude and love was catching to anyone open to experience it. Many accepted the small things in life with joy and enthusiasm.

Maggie, Deborah, Sarina, and Janette sat at the long table selecting Bible verses they should teach the girls. They needed passages about planting and preparing herbs and vegetables. They emptied the Bible coffer, laid all the papyri on the table, and scanned them for passages on dietary laws. Sarina found a stiff, little used, scroll at the bottom of the chest. "What a lonely, neglected little scroll. It hasn't had much attention."

Janette resisted the diversion because she was concentrating on Leviticus, "Then it probably doesn't have what we're looking for."

Curious, Sarina laid it on the table. It was inflexible and difficult to open. Her attempts to unroll it caused crumbling. Deborah got a wet towel to help. From the other side of the table, she dampened the papyrus to make it resilient and keep it intact. It stubbornly sprang back to its original rounded position when she tried to spread it. It wasn't pliant like the others. Sarina smoothed it out slowly until she was able to hold the ends in place. "It's just eight chapters."

She read the title, "Song of Songs."

Maggie grinned, "It must be a great song then. Let's hear it."

"'Your lips cover me with kisses; your love is better than wine.'"

That got Janette's attention, "It's love poetry?"

Deborah was confused, "We haven't heard this in the synagogue."

"Or at home either," Maggie added.

"Wonder why it's in this box with Biblical scrolls?" Sarina mused with a frown. She let it roll back up.

"It's not about dietary laws," Deborah agreed. "That's for sure."

Sarina dismissed it, "Well, it's not appropriate for our girls."

"Oh no you don't," Janette said pulling the ends back out. "What else does it say?"

Sarina continued to read, "'Take me with you, and we'll run away; be my king and take me to your room. We will be happy together, drink deep, and lose ourselves in love.'"

Maggie was astounded, "Be my king? She wants him to rule her?"

"It was written by a woman?" Deborah asked, puzzled, "But men do all the writing."

Janette read ahead. "Look at this ninth verse. 'You, my love, excite men as a mare excites the stallions of Pharaoh's chariots.' Sounds sexy."

Maggie crowded between Sarina and Janette. "'He lies upon my breasts.' It could be about a newborn son suckling his mother."

Deborah read upside down from the other side of the table. "I don't think so. 'I am weak from passion. His left hand is under my head, and his right hand caresses me.'"

Edita walked in. The girls plopped down onto the bench and the scroll sprang back to its cylindrical position. "What's going on? You girls look like you're up to something."

Deborah rose to take part of the foodstuffs that Edita was carrying. "No. We were just absorbed in Leviticus, looking for verses about food. You scared us because we didn't expect you."

Deborah diverted Edita's attention by helping her put away her purchases while Maggie grabbed the interesting scroll and stuffed it into the large pocket of her sleeve. "I'm going to get something at Dora's. Are the rest of you coming?" They left hurriedly, not wanting to be left behind.

Edita frowned at the table. It was scattered with loose papyri in various stages of open and rolled. She shook her head to adjust, not sure of what just happened. The young women were here one moment and gone the next.

They rushed giggling and hooting to the hut. Dora wasn't surprised to see them come in, but they usually knocked first and it was unusual for them to be wound up, gather around her table, and carefully unwind a scroll.

Janette sat in front of the scroll, "Look at this. 'I found him. I held him and wouldn't let him go until I took him to my mother's house, to the room where I was born.'"

Dora put a fresh pot of water on the fire. They would need tea for this.

Janette read an even more shocking passage, "'Your breasts are like gazelles.'"

Deborah was puzzled, "How can breasts be like gazelles?"

Maggie traced the simile, "Gazelles are fast and graceful."

"I don't think breasts are fast," Sarina said, shaking her head. "I don't even think they can be graceful."

Janette didn't want to stop reading in order to debate, "What do you think this means? 'I will stay on the hill of myrrh, the hill of incense.'"

"I see! Hills look like breasts," Sarina said, knowing what Janette was thinking.

"It could be a metaphor," Deborah said.

"It's all metaphors," Maggie agreed.

Janette gave her voice a dramatic character, "'The taste of honey is on your lips, my darling; your tongue is milk and honey for me.'"

Dora poured tea.

Maggie giggled as she sipped. "I have that feeling between my legs like I do when Ephraim rears up on a ewe."

Dora wanted them to understand, "When you think of romance, your insides feel soft and stimulated. Romance makes your juices flow in anticipation of making love with your mate. This poetry incites those feelings in you."

Janette was wound up, "'Let my lover come to my garden and eat the best of its fruits.'"

Maggie tried to translate the metaphor, "The best of its fruits? The woman is the fruit and she wants him to eat her?"

Dora held her cup calmly, worldly wise as the situation demanded. "Yes. That's an erotic way of making love."

Janette was caught up in fantasy, staring into space. Deborah continued the reading. "Then the man says, 'I am eating my honey and honeycomb; I am drinking my wine and milk.'"

"Erotic again. He's lapping up her love juices."

Even Janette was shocked. "Oooh, that's repulsive."

Dora calmly took a sip of tea. "Maybe so, but it's pleasurable."

Deborah made her voice a low whisper, quivering amorously, "'I am trembling; you have made me as eager for love as a chariot driver is for battle.'"

Not inclined to drama, Sarina's voice had a matter of fact tone, "'Your breasts are clusters of grapes.'"

Maggie hooted at the idea of bunches of grapes hanging from a woman's chest. It was a silly, distracting metaphor.

"Where did this scroll come from?" Dora asked.

"It was in the bottom of the Bible coffer."

"Oh, I see."

Maggie was impressed at Dora's wide knowledge once again. She only hoped to develop half of Dora's wisdom. "You do?"

"It's the Song of Songs. It's part of the Bible."

Deborah's naiveté was being shattered, "Really?"

"I don't believe that." Sarina was unwilling to let go of her black and white categories for viewing life.

Maggie scoffed, "The synagogue teaches that sex is sinful while this is in the Bible!"

Dora could see it was going to take more than reading romantic poetry for them to adjust their thinking. They were mature enough to give up literal concepts and enter the realm of ambiguity. She would help them see things another way. "Sex is a part of life. Without it, we couldn't have children and there would be no more people. It makes no sense that something so necessary could be sinful."

Deborah sifted through her confusion, "I just thought parents were ashamed of it. They don't talk about it. They hide it. They won't let us talk about it or even think it."

"Sex is a private thing," Sarina said defending the custom.

"Not in the fields," Maggie said. "Sheep do it out in the open. It's not a big deal to them. They do it any time while they go about their other business."

"But people try not to let others know when they're having sex," Sarina countered.

Janette held nothing back, "If you get pregnant, then everybody knows." She wasn't as proper as Sarina.

Sarina moved from doubt to practicality, "Then you have to find a way to take care of the baby."

Dora agreed this should be about more than sex, "We wait until we're committed to one person and prepare by establishing a home."

Janette showed her bawdiness again. "That's the reason we built houses for Leora and Samuel then Batia and Dan, so they would have a private place for sex." She expected everyone to laugh, but they were only shocked.

Dora reined it back in, "I don't think I want to express it in that raw way. That makes it seem that marriage is just for sex."

Sarina said, "It's for having children." She knew why people got married.

"It's a sacred act to establish a safe space for a family to love and grow," Dora continued. "We go to great lengths to sanctify intimacy between a man and woman with a ceremony before God and man. Couples go to the marriage bed in complete awareness of the covenant they are sharing with the blessing and approval of their parents, family, friends, and God."

Janette noticed worldly ways, "That's different from the harlots that live by the walls."

"We shouldn't judge the harlots. Many are forced into that way of life because we don't care for the widows and dispossessed. Harlotry gives them a way to take care of themselves."

"How can they live with themselves?" Sarina tried to understand. "Aren't they ashamed?"

"I think most are. Others accept their lot and become hardened to the ways of the world. You can see it on their faces. Notice it the next time you see them in the market."

Deborah felt compassion for the prostitutes, "That is so sad, being used by so many men on demand."

Janette judged the men, "Men who go to the harlots are not attractive, or they would have their own woman."

"Some men are though. Some are kind. Prostitutes rejoice when they find the favor of a kind man."

Sarina thought that unlikely, "How can he be kind if he makes someone have sex with him who doesn't want to?"

"Most of them want to because they need the money."

Deborah's sympathy shifted to the men, "Isn't it degrading for him to pay for love?"

"Only the young and naïve expect a whore to love them. They just pay to have their sexual urges satisfied."

Sarina tried to make sense of this, "So men are satisfied to have sex without love?"

Maggie was willing to push old concepts aside, "You have only to watch sheep to know sex has nothing to do with love."

"The ram just wants it and climbs on the first ewe he sees in heat," Dora explained.

Janette was puzzled, "In heat?"

"That means she's ready to get pregnant," Maggie said.

"How does he know?" Janette asked.

Dora mentored them, "She has a smell that attracts him."

"Is that why women wear perfume?" Janette wanted to know.

"Yes, but many don't know that's why."

Deborah knew why she wore perfume. It had nothing to do with getting a man. "They just don't want to smell bad. They want to smell good."

"Dora?" Maggie hesitated.

Dora waited for what she knew would be a difficult question.

"Dora?" The other girls looked at her curiously.

"Dora, you make perfumes. Do you make them smell like women are in heat?"

"There are special ingredients that can do that, but women have a special smell when they are ready to become pregnant like ewes do."

"How do we know if we're in heat?" Janette asked bluntly.

"You'll get sexually excited more easily at that time of the month."

"Every month?"

"Yes, it's midway between your menses. If you're in your period during the wane of the moon, you're ripe during the full moon.

Sarina's mind was in its logical mode, "And if you bleed during the full moon, you're ripe at waning. That means we all have to figure it out for ourselves. Does everyone know this?"

Janette looked at Dora over her cup.

"Most go by instinct. I learned because I'm a midwife."

Maggie saw possibilities in this, "That means that there is a time when women don't get pregnant."

"They don't get pregnant during or close to their bloodletting."

Sarina questioned the Law's practically, "But Leviticus says a woman is ritually unclean during her loss of blood and men are not to have intercourse with their wives then."

Janette voiced what the others were thinking. "So if they don't have sex midway between periods and only when it is close to their menses, they can't get pregnant."

"We're teachers. We can tell young girls," Maggie said, altruistic.

"You have to be careful what you tell the girls. You might get in trouble if their parents find out."

"Girls need to know this," insisted Maggie.

Sarina agreed it was dangerous, "Then they will think it's okay to have sex close to their period."

"But it would empower them to know when they can have sex without getting pregnant," Maggie defended.

Janette saw the advantage, "Then they can please their men without fear of consequences."

But it wasn't practical to Sarina. "What if men aren't attracted to them because they aren't in heat?"

"Oh, men are always drawn to the woman they want. And women primp to make themselves beautiful and use perfumes to attract their men because they desire them."

Sarina wasn't sure about this, "Women desire men?"

Janette couldn't believe Sarina didn't know, "Sure they do. Just as much as men desire them, sometimes even more."

Maggie saw what went on in some homes she visited with Dora. "Some women sleep in the room with their daughters to avoid their men so they won't get pregnant."

Dora shook her head, "It's a sad thing to evade your man. Then he may be tempted to go elsewhere."

"You mean to the prostitutes," Janette concluded.

"The law says, 'Wives submit to your husbands,'" Deborah remembered. "Does that mean to give them sex when they want it?"

"Some say it also means to obey your husband. But there's more to sex than having children and being afraid of getting pregnant. The Song of Songs is about romantic love, not just sex. The couple is deeply in love and enamored of one another. They convey their fascination with each other with fantasy and metaphors. Each tells the other how they make them feel."

Janette was open to that idea, "I would love for someone to feel that way about me."

The others felt it too, but were too timid to say it out loud.

"I hope that all of you find a man who uplifts you."

Dora refilled everyone's cup with hot tea.

"Young people need to understand the repercussions and rewards of making love. Their physical bodies have a primordial urge to mate. They are attracted to someone, their energies stir to merge with that person. It's exciting and brings great pleasure, particularly at climax. But when a maiden shares sex with a man, she absorbs his unresolved issues – anger, fear, frustration, greed - and he takes hers. They also take on the other's joy, peace, and love. If the girl wants more than a physical relationship and the boy does not, she can feel disappointed at what she perceives as rejection.

"It's tougher on the female if she becomes pregnant. It's easier for the man to walk away than for her. But the energy exchange has taken place. The allusion in the wedding ceremony to man and wife becoming one is very literal in a spiritual sense.

"This energy isn't physical. It cannot be perceived by the senses. You can't see, hear, smell, taste, or touch it. It's spiritual, beyond the sensual experience of making love. You create an energy field with the man. Think of your aura as a bowl of water. Suppose the man had a bowl of grape juice and a woman has orange juice. He puts drops of grape juice in her bowl, and she puts drops of orange juice in his. The purple and orange colors of the juices swirl around each other at first and eventually merge to form another color, of a slightly different flavor. They have the qualities of the original substance, but mix to form something else.

"The energy field of a person is around and through them in the shape of a large egg. When a man and woman join their auras through making love, they share all their energies, the good along with the bad. One must select carefully when deciding to share their selves.

"The physical bodies remain intact and unchanged. Of course, young virgins lose their virginity or any female may become pregnant. There's more at stake for the female than the male. There is real power behind sexuality. It isn't a toy. It takes us beyond time and space for a glorious, holy instant."

CHAPTER 11

Maggie put her stuff away and was weaving when Lizette burst in, "What did he say?"

Maggie looked at her with a puzzled frown. What was Lizette talking about?

"You just walked all the way home with Raamah."

"No, I didn't. He followed me home."

"Well?"

"Well? Well what?"

"What did he say?"

"Nothing much. Just small talk."

"Well, it wasn't about you. The two of you hate each other."

Maggie agreed, "It's strange. He was actually nice."

"Did he ask about me?"

"No, why would he ask me about you?"

"I want him to notice me."

Despite Maggie's own aversion to Raamah, Lizette had a crush on him. "He's always noticed me and, believe me, it is not a good thing."

"You provoke him."

"He provokes me."

"Well next time he's provoking you, put in a good word for me."

"Help me with the girls tomorrow," Maggie said thoughtfully.

Lizette gave her a conspirator's smile, "Okay, see you then." She bounded out as suddenly as she arrived.

When Maggie and Lizette arrived the next day, they put down their stuff and placed their feet wide apart to brace themselves so they wouldn't lose their balance due to the onslaught of childish hugs around their legs. They returned the hugs until the girls let go, satisfied the counselors reciprocated their love. As they settled in a circle around the sand, mothers waved and left to do morning chores, shop in the market, escort boys to school. Some sat on a cluster of benches to embroider in the plaza.

Maggie and Lizette sang a Psalm of praise with the girls. Then Maggie kneeled to show them how to make their letters. Copying her, they etched in the sand, then sang songs and played games about the letters. She loved their whimsical nature and their eagerness to learn. They closed the lesson with a Psalm of thanks. Each girl left with a final hug and she swept away their etchings and poured water over the area to repack the sand.

Lizette surreptitiously glanced around for Raamah as she helped Maggie clear up. She wore a light scent of lavender and her best everyday tunic. She pinched her cheeks to a blushing pink and had applied kohl lightly around her eyes. Maggie approved of her efforts. ~Good. That'll make me look drab beside her. Raamah will notice her instead of me. I just hope he shows up today.~

Maggie needn't have worried. Raamah waited by the gate. He walked alongside them and offered to carry Maggie's harp. She quickly excused herself, "Thank you, no. I have to hurry home. I promised to help Papa. Would you walk Lizette home?"

She smiled at Lizette, "I'll see you tomorrow." Lizette smiled back and squeezed her hand gratefully.

Maggie quickened her pace. It was her turn to take the sheep out today.

While tending the flock, she reviewed the day. She loved what she did with the girls. They were a joy to work with. Her interplay with them invigorated rather than tired her, and she could do anything. She basked in their innocent adoration, was exhilarated by their love and youthful enthusiasm. When she went to the market, girls ran to hug her. She didn't even have to be a good teacher. They learned naturally. All she had to do was return their love.

Maggie thought Lizette and Raamah were making progress. Maggie walked with them sometimes, but was always careful to leave them alone. She begged off because of errands, promises to meet friends, or to go on rounds with Dora. She insisted on going to her house first, leaving Raamah to walk the rest of the way with Lizette.

On this day, Lizette went into Maggie's house with her. They fell into an easy rhythm as they cooked together, one seasoning the lamb, the other preparing vegetables.

"I don't think Raamah is ever going to like me," Lizette said, woefully.

"Of course he likes you. Who wouldn't? You talk and laugh together. Obviously you both enjoy yourselves."

"True," Lizette tore a leaf of chard into a bowl of vegetables, "But we're friends. He doesn't see me as anything else." She deftly sliced a cucumber into the mix.

"I don't see why not. You're attractive, smart, and fun," Maggie rubbed olive oil on the lamb's surface, "I'll walk with him tomorrow and make him think of you differently. You go on ahead and I'll tell him you had to walk some girls home. I'll talk to him then."

Maggie sat at the potter's wheel throwing bottles for Dora's concoctions. She would etch names of herbs on them. They would make Dora's shelves neater and she would love them.

She didn't know what she would tell Raamah about Lizette. She had come to the shop hoping the monotony would let her thoughts run wild. It would be easy to point out Lizette's physical attributes. No one could miss those. Men and boys, even women, unwittingly stared at her natural beauty. Surely, Raamah knew her great personality. They had walked together for weeks. Maybe he didn't know Lizette's intelligence and cleverness.

Good. Perhaps she would talk to him about Lizette's accomplishments, her great ideas, and her graciousness.

~Maybe he's aware of all that, but hasn't shown an interest in her because she intimidates him. Only a youth of great confidence would be courageous enough to approach Lizette. She is so beautiful they probably think she has many suitors. They're afraid of the competition.

~But that shouldn't be a problem for Raamah. He's more arrogant than anyone. What is it then?

~Maybe he only needs to know Lizette's interested in him.~

She stared at the wheel as it slowed down. ~That could be it! Men often can't see the obvious. Raamah has spent enough time with Lizette to know her attractions. He just needs help to think of her as a potential mate. As a woman, Lizette can't approach him with her amorous interests. He's the man. It's up to him, but he needs a little push.

~Men always want what they can't have. Lizette needs to stay away from him a while so he will miss her and realize life is better with her around.~

Raamah was pleased to see Maggie coming the next day without her usual companion.

Maggie was ready. She was tired of Raamah hassling her. He knew she didn't want him to trail her. She wanted it to stop at once. Lizette liked him. He was supposed to fall for her. Maggie didn't like him at all. She waited in the middle of the road to tell him so. She faced him with her hands on her hips, but he stepped into her space. From his tallness, he saw the top of her wavy copper hair and scarcely noticed her indignant stance. When she looked up into his eyes to give him a piece of her mind, he was intrigued by her dark eyebrows and scintillating eyes, made all the more fascinating by her rage.

She was startled by what she saw in his eyes. Where she expected to see disdain, she saw respect and admiration. ~Oh, my God!~

He stroked her hair and teased, "Why did you stop?"

~Why did I stop? I forgot. Did I need to go back and get something?~ She mentally checked the things she was carrying. Her harp! "I forgot my harp." She turned to go back for it.

"Maggie." She kept going. She wasn't going to stop for him again.

"Maggie."

He ran to catch up with her. He passed her and walked backward to face her.

"Maggie, I have your harp," he said, holding it up for her to see.

She looked at it, puzzled.

"I'm carrying it for you."

How could she have gotten so confused? "Of course you do. What did I forget?"

"Nothing. You have everything."

She turned toward home again. He turned with her. They walked in silence, both of their minds racing: She, wondering at the change in him, and he delighted at his effect on her. She, not believing it, he hoping she would see they were meant for each other.

~Oh my!~ she thought, ~He doesn't hate me. What am I going to do? He likes me instead of Lizette. We've sent him the wrong message. How are we going to make him realize it's Lizette he really wants?~

It was a quiet walk home. Maggie's discomfort grew.

"Give it to me!"

"Give it to you?"

"Yes, my harp. Give it to me."

He sighed patiently, "Maggie, it's no trouble. I want to carry it for you."

"Don't be nice to me ever again. I'll carry my own harp."

He was obliged let her have it.

As she walked away in a huff, he noticed the tenseness in her back, how stiff she held her neck and shoulders.

After she went several steps, she heard him whistle a happy little tune. She turned in time to see him click his heels and walk jauntily up the road.

He was amused that he made her nervous!

She groaned. She had forgotten to talk about Lizette. How could she have bungled it so badly?

Lizette burst into Enoch's shop anxious to learn what had happened. She halted when she saw Maggie's morose demeanor.

"What's wrong?"

Maggie put down her stylus. Dora's bottles would have to wait. "I don't understand it. Raamah likes me."

Lizette was stunned. She sat down on the stool beside Maggie's work bench.

Maggie looked down at the unfinished bottles. "I didn't get to tell him he should pursue you. He acted like a suitor."

"What did he say?"

"Nothing. I didn't give him a chance. I told him not to ever be nice to me again."

Lizette took a deep breath.

Maggie wallowed in guilt and self-pity.

Lizette sensed her despair, "Maggie, it's not your fault. You tried. I tried. He's not attracted to me. He wants you. Besides, I don't want someone who doesn't want me. I'll find someone someday." She didn't like for Maggie to feel bad. "Izaak walked me home today," she said.

Maggie brightened at Lizette's hope of finding happiness, "You should encourage him. Maybe Raamah will see what he's missing and be jealous."

"Oh Maggie, don't you see? He won't notice. He loves you." She hugged her friend and touched her cheek, "I want you to be happy. I want him to be happy too. The two of you can be happy together."

Maggie was unwilling to admit defeat. She would get Lizette and Raamah together one way or another.

Her heart fell when she got back to the house. Eban was visiting her father. She went into the kitchen to help Edita and Sarina prepare supper. She tried to hear the conversation outside the window, but Enoch and Eban talked in low tones and the clatter of pots, pans, and kitchen utensils muffled what she might hear.

She didn't dare ask Edita what was going on. The girls, Ximena and Chanda, still wove on the veranda outside the kitchen and would hear if the women talked. If they whispered, the men would notice hushed sounds from the kitchen and suspect they were speculating.

Eban was priest. He didn't visit people. He left that for Zadika and his minions. Only one thing would bring Eban out of his palatial mansion into the streets of Magdala. He looked for a bride for his son. She was sure of it. Instead of imagining another reason for his visit, she would wait for him to leave and get the real answer from her father.

She automatically did her usual chores while her mother and sister did theirs. Her preoccupation was hidden behind Sarina's enthusiasm for the weaving she had done with the girls that day. The verandah was scattered with specimens of youthful weaving in progress. The girls were proud of their cloths. Some were doing advanced projects. The most proficient were staying late in their fervor to complete sections of their design.

After Eban left and the last girl had gone home with her brother, the family sat down to supper. The usual banter was absent from the table. Anticipating an announcement, they passed food and poured water without comment. They ate because the food was ready and it was time. They all knew Eban had been there and something important was eminent. Enoch would tell them, but they knew he would wait until they finished eating.

At last, Enoch put down his fork and cleared his throat. The family waited expectantly.

"As you know, Eban, the priest, came to visit me this afternoon."

Edita lowered her glass, "Most unusual for the priest to visit. Was he requesting your help?"

"You might say that. He wishes to betroth his son, Raamah, to Maggie."

Edita felt like she had been hit. She wasn't prepared for the revelation. Enoch didn't consult her. She didn't have time to decide how she felt about the matter or how to respond. Enoch's unilateral action threw her off balance. They usually discussed important matters and presented a united front.

Everyone turned to Maggie wearing tentative smiles.

Maggie slammed down her fork in frustration, "No!" She buried her face in her hands. She had feared this when she saw Eban on the front stoop, but that didn't lessen her dismay at the revelation. She would get out of this some way.

Sarina tried to be glad for her, "Congratulations, Maggie. Raamah's a good catch."

"I don't want to marry Raamah, Lizette wants to marry him."

"Maggie, he isn't asking for Lizette," Enoch said. "He's asking for you. I thought you would be thrilled. I've seen you walk with him after club meetings. I assumed your childhood rivalry is over and you are friends now."

"Not really, he's been pursuing me and I've been trying to help Lizette's case. I wouldn't walk with him if it weren't for her."

"Let Lizette find her own suitor, she's not your responsibility."

Maggie wept, "But Lizette wants him, and she's my friend!"

"Well, he's asked for you," Enoch said, appealing to her obedience. "Forget about Lizette's interest in him and give him a chance."

"Why did Eban ask for me for his son? He is a priest. Raamah will be a priest. He should marry the daughter of a wealthy man. Papa, I can't believe Eban is going to allow his son to marry the daughter of a potter and sheep herder."

That made no sense to Batia, "You underestimate yourselves. Everyone knows that Mama Edita and Papa Enoch are respected by the leaders of the synagogue. We follow the law and contribute faithfully. Samuel reads the lesson most Sabbaths. He and Dan distinguished themselves in the school. Dan is becoming chazzan. Leora and Mama are leaders among women. You and Sarina have a following of girls and their families. We are a good family, Maggie."

Edita concurred, "If we didn't know that, we do now. Otherwise, Eban would not have asked for you."

"I'm not surprised," Dan opined, "Raamah's been crazy about you ever since you first started playing stickball."

"He hated me! He tormented me and made fun of me. He was jealous of me!"

"That's all true. He was attracted to you. How else could he hide it from himself?"

Maggie groaned, "If he's hiding it from himself, how does he know?"

"Maybe he couldn't keep from thinking about you," Batia said.

Sarina sighed, "It's quite romantic really. Do you think about him all the time?"

"No." She gave it more thought. She did think about him a lot. "Well maybe, but only because he irritates me."

Dan gestured toward her, "See who else is in denial."

"When you walk together, you seem to get along," Batia said.

"That's because I'm trying to make him like Lizette. It's not for me."

Edita put a second helping of lamb on her plate, "Sounds like you've been unavailable. Men want what they can't have."

Maggie grasped at this straw, "It's true isn't it, Papa? He can't have me. Can he?"

"It's a good match. You'll live in the palace and have servants to help you with your projects. You like Zadika. You can help her with the poor and sick. Raamah will be priest. You'll bring him the support of the women and girls. You might be able to start a real school with his assistance."

Maggie thought it maddening that Enoch had not given a direct answer, but she began to consider the possibilities. The girls' club was the source of much controversy. The girls loved it. One, Ximena, had been guarded at first. She only followed directions reluctantly and withheld her enthusiasm the first couple of months. But having woven at home, she was won over by weaving with Sarina and had become fascinated with writing. She had even found ways to include words in her weaving. When she took her finished product home and gave it to her mother, her father was scandalized. He was disturbed that his daughter knew how to form letters and asked her where she learned such foolishness. When he found that the girls' club was responsible, he tried to put a stop to it. He talked to other fathers who formed a delegation and went the priest. Eban was appalled.

When the counselors learned from the girls what their fathers were up to, they met to devise a plan of action. Should they stop the girls' club, scale back to baby-sitting, or continue in the face of scandal? They decided to stand firm and look for support.

Maggie went to Zadika, the one person who could influence Eban, and laid their activities bare before her. Zadika loved what they were doing. She became a sponsor and joined them one morning a week to establish a visible presence of support from the priesthood.

Yes, Maggie had reason to appreciate Zadika and wanted to please her. Zadika grew more and more attached to Maggie, the counselors, and the girls. Eban wasn't pleased, but he truly loved Zadika and didn't want to go against her. The club was sanctioned. Then Ximena forgot her initial skepticism and became an avid follower, devoted to the counselors, sponsors, and the club.

Maggie reluctantly resigned herself to the betrothal. Raamah wasn't so bad when he was being nice. And what other options did she have? She could herd and heal and do her projects, but those were always the same. The girls' club was her avenue of expansion. She could make the world a better place one girl at a time. Each of them would marry and teach their girls and a network of capable, educated women would grow.

That would happen more easily with the support of the clergy and the elders. Betrothed to Raamah, she could permanently foster that reinforcement. If she turned down Raamah's suit, would Zadika still champion the club? She didn't want to lose Zadika's support.

The betrothal ceremony was a blur. Maggie put on a sunny smile and looked into Raamah's eyes, not allowing her thoughts to acknowledge her fear and dread. She concentrated on her vision of using the palace as her base of operation for the girls' club. Raamah stared at her in his dark, intense way while she drew comfort from his handsome face and adoring eyes. She saw love and trust there. Confidence. He was sure of her, even if she wasn't sure of him. She felt like a princess, not believing that her dreams were coming true. But it wasn't her dream. She had never dreamed this. Was it possible his love would be enough for both of them?

Dan played his harp while the girls sang praises to God for the creation of the earth in Psalm 104. Together, Edita and Zadika forcefully threw a cloth wrapped ceramic plate against the rock courtyard. With this, Maggie's fate was sealed. The betrothal was final, just as a broken plate was final. It couldn't be repaired and neither party could renege. She accepted it, convinced it would be a good life.

Maggie's friends and neighbors celebrated in the garden with a feast in the couple's honor. Full of food and wine and tired of the jubilant atmosphere, she left the crowd for a few moments of privacy.

A thick cloth attracted her attention when she went by the items from the betrothal ceremony. Curious, she moved the cloth away. It was the plate! ~The betrothal plate didn't break. Is it a sign?~ She looked around, saw she was alone, covered it again, and took it to the room she shared with Sarina. She placed it in her chest beneath her linens.

Her doubts returned. Was she doing the right thing? She packed her sheep herding supplies: her boy's clothes, strong sandals, staff, water skin, harp, slingshot, dagger, embroidery project, and pouch of herbs. She hid them under her bed so she could get them quickly.

She went back to join the festivities. When everyone left, she went directly to bed for a good night's rest.

When sleep eluded her, she rose and furtively retrieved her supplies. Sarina was fast asleep. Careful not to awaken anyone, she passed through the kitchen to pack food left from the feast then went to the sheep in the barn. Bo and Abbe quietly came to her for affection. Well trained and obedient, they didn't balk when she opened the gate, and followed when she led the flock down the road. She needed time away from the demands of the life she had made.

Grazing was sparse in local fields from lack of rain. The sheep needed time in distant, fresh fields so that local pastures could revive.

She would have time alone to think and listen to the voice for God. Maybe the most obvious path was not the best one.

She led them north to the Plain of Gennesaret where fertile fields were fed by mountain springs flowing toward the Sea of Galilee. Travelers would not find it strange that a shepherd moved his flock in the cool of the early morning, before the road was crowded.

Thick fog joined Maggie's bleak thoughts. It hung low over the Sea of Galilee on her right. The closest sheep blurred in the mist and she only dimly saw the last of her flock behind her. But she trusted Abbe and Bo to keep them together and kept a steady pace, slow enough to accommodate the smallest lambs. The fog pressed down upon her dreary mind. The weather wallowed with her in depression, infecting the sheep. She herded a mass of murkiness down the road.

Preoccupied with her racing thoughts, she hardly missed a step when she picked up a small lamb that fell behind. The dogs chased stray lambs and coaxed them back to the flock. How she had missed her times with the animals! Life was simple with them. Protect them. Lead them to green pastures. Watch their playful antics. Observe their instincts.

At first light, she passively noticed fishermen shoving their boats into the water. It was the kind of day that fish were likely to bite. Fishermen took advantage of it. She envied their simple life.

Sheep were like children if you really thought about it. It was adults who were complicated with dreams and devious schemes to make them come true. Adults thought they could only get what they wanted by doing what others wanted or by persuading someone else to do things their way. ~We're all intertwined, and should fit together perfectly like the pieces of a puzzle.~

When she could make out the shapes of objects on the side of the road, she paused under an olive tree to let the sheep graze in a grassy area and ate sparingly of lamb from the betrothal feast.

~Sheep are nonchalant. They ignore others and go about their own business. When they are ready, they fall in line with others or others join them. It's just a matter of patience and flexibility.

~I'm patiently waiting for my dreams to come true. Yes, I'm being flexible. If dreams don't come true the way I want, I accept them in the way they come.

She relished the mutton from the feast. It was as tender and tasty as the night before.

~Sheep do not try to make others stop what they are doing. Not unless the others bother them, anyway.

~Have I bothered anyone, really? Why do the elders care whether girls read and write? Who does that hurt? The men are unsure of their power if they fear for a few women to read. How disgusting that such cowards are in charge!~

She thanked the tree and the food, and then took up her staff to lead her flock.

~And I'm caught in the intrigue, not really trying to please, but trying to make it look like I'm pleasing so I can continue doing what I want. Thank goodness there are others who also want what I want.~

She stashed her supplies when she got to the valley. The flock spread and rushed to the fertile field. She hurried to keep them from making themselves sick by gorging themselves on the abundant clover. She had to keep them together. She shouted an order to Bo and Abbe and they circled the flock to reinforce the boundaries. When they were contained, she sang soothing songs to slow their grazing. She spent the afternoon helping the flock adjust to the green pastures. A few contrary wethers tested the borders and the dogs coaxed those castrated ones back to the grazing area.

The women of Magdala knew how to insist on what they wanted. Some withheld their favors until their men relented. Others went on strike: refused to cook or make their favorite meals, refused to clean house, let their men's clothes stay dirty. They used the ways of women throughout the ages to exert influence over men. They also rewarded their men to make them happy when they were pleased by them.

She supposed she would to do that with Raamah. As bizarre as it seemed, Zadika probably withheld her favors to control Eban. A man like him had servants to do the domestic chores, so she couldn't have much control over his food, clothing, and shelter. Though it was hard to imagine either one of them copulating, Zadika must be a sex kitten to have such profound influence over Eban. Will I have to be sexy like her? It amused Maggie to think of herself in that way.

Satisfied the flock was controlled, she moved her supplies to a shade where she ate a late lunch.

Or maybe Eban thrived on Zadika's overflowing goodness and didn't want to disturb it by going against her.

She walked around the sheep.

Maybe it wasn't that pleasant for Eban. Maggie didn't trust him. He might be reluctant to bend to Zadika's will. Maybe she knows something he doesn't want revealed. A past indiscretion, a secret concubine. Maggie didn't want to speculate on what it could be.

She led the flock to the river to quench their thirst and fill her water skin.

Her parents had a healthy relationship based on love, respect, and trust. They talked openly and freely with each other and made decisions together. Each tried to do more for the other than the other did for them. Would she ever be able to have that with Raamah? In that respect, she and Raamah were from two different worlds.

She left her supplies in the mouth of a cave by the river and went to play with the lambs.

Maggie was determined to do what she had to do to get what she really wanted. What was that? What did she really want?

To make a difference? Did that include marriage? Not necessarily.

The sheep rested content in the soft grass. She laughed at a small lamb running after a butterfly.

She thought of the stability of the girls' club and the possibility of starting an actual school. Would marriage to Raamah get her what she really wanted?

It most certainly would. She would make sure it did even if she had to sacrifice and compromise.

Resolving to go through with it, she practiced hitting the trunk of a tree with rocks from her slingshot.

The next day passed like the one before. She loved her idyllic pastoral surroundings and surrendered to the monotony of shepherding. The scorching sun beat down on the fields. The song birds flew over her healthy flock. The river flowed gently in the valley beyond the waving grass.

She absorbed herself in a bucolic existence with only animals to keep her company. Nothing was more important than nurturing the flock, eating on schedule, and languishing in the river. There wasn't a cleaner stream on earth. It was so clear she could see ochre, coral, white, and grey pebbles magnified in the water, worn smooth at the bottom of the stream. But cold, the coldest thing she had ever felt. She kept her vegetables fresh in a basket in the water. No need to dry them in the sun. Cold, refreshing water to drink. When she was hot in the field, she poured cold, clear water over her head from her water skin. Water was easily accessible with the running river, not like the wadis[1] near Magdala at this time of year. She dangled her feet in the water and walked in the running stream in her clothes, rinsing them off while she washed away the dust and sweat on her body. Then she let them dry in the hot sun while she lay on a smooth rock.

She lost track of the days for they were all alike. When the betrothal food was gone, she stood still in the water until the fish forgot about her and she was able to catch them in her hands. Trees hung over the river and wild grape vines draped down for her to swing on.

After a fortnight, she heard the 'Song of Praise to the Earth' beneath the cacophony of nature sounds and recognized Dan's voice in the distance. At some level, she had known he would come after her. She was ready for him. She had thought things through and was prepared to leave the cocoon she had made for herself.

Bo and Abbe met him barking, tails wagging excitedly. She waited and let him come to her. The dogs were wound up. He ruffled their fur and threw a ball ahead of him. They competed to reach the ball first and take it back to him. He threw out another for Abbe when Bo beat her to the first one, then threw Bo's out again when he brought it back.

Maggie exulted at the innocent game and Dan's playfulness. She wondered if Raamah had that in him. Maybe he did. He could certainly play stickball.

Dan smiled down at her when he finally reached her, "Looks like you're doing very well." He held up a bag full of food. "I brought provisions. Maybe you and the dogs have eaten all the betrothal food by now."

She grinned back at him. He didn't have to know of the conflict within her soul. It embarrassed her.

"Yep." She led him to the mouth of the cave where they partook of bread, fresh fruit, leftover fish, and vegetables.

"Did anyone worry about me?"

---

[1] a dry riverbed that contains water only during times of heavy rain

"Not any of us. We know you well. Raamah, however…"

"Oh no! I hope he didn't take this personally."

"He did at first, but we assured him you went to pasture the sheep and that we knew about it."

"You lied for me?"

"Not really. As you remember, we did talk of going. We just expected it to be me or Papa. You settled it by taking things into your own hands."

They took turns sipping from his wine skin.

"We told Raamah that we assumed the two of you had talked about it. When he said you had not, we said, 'She's been so busy with arrangements for the betrothal that she probably thought she had.'"

He bit into an apple and chewed thoughtfully, "He was going to rush off to find you."

"What? He's never been in the pasture. How would he know how to find me? He doesn't know how to take care of himself in the wild."

"I know. I don't think he realizes how difficult it can be. It looks easy to most people. They don't understand that it takes special skills. He doesn't know your capabilities."

"But you're here. That means you were able to convince him."

"Yes, I know you wanted to be alone, Maggie, but the only way I could convince him to stay was to come after you myself. He was determined to come with me. I thought it better that he stay home."

"You didn't come right away. It wouldn't take a fortnight for you to get here."

"I did leave, immediately. I just took a detour."

"What did you do, go fishing?"

He laughed, "Yes. Samuel took me with him in his boat on the sea. He dropped me off at the Plain of Gennesaret."

He threw his apple core into the river and watched it float downstream.

"Did you need time away from Raamah, Maggie?"

Maggie took a deep breath, "Yes. Everything happened so fast. I didn't have time to adjust to what was happening."

"And?"

"I've thought it through. I'm all right now."

Seemingly satisfied, Dan walked around the flock checking for health or injuries. Maggie sang with her harp, calming them after the excitement of being with their master again. A few of the ewes wandered over to rub against him.

They settled into regular shifts of sleep and tending the sheep. Maggie had slept while the dogs watched. Their animal instincts were ever alert for predators. But she had interrupted her nights to check the flock. With Dan there, she could sleep without interruptions.

Both were competent shepherds but it was much easier to work with a partner. When he was asleep and it was her turn to watch the sheep, her thoughts ran rampant. Dan sensed her need to be isolated and left her alone as much as possible. They had their meals together.

"Do you love Raamah?"

Ugh! She felt like he had hit her in the gut. She looked away to avoid meeting his eyes.

"I don't know."

"Surely you have feelings for him or you wouldn't have agreed to marry him."

She shifted on the rock. "Yes, I do," she admitted, "But I don't know whether I hate him or love him."

"It can be hard to tell the difference. At least there's passion between you. It'll never be dull."

"It might not be exactly what I want, and I have a longing for something different. I don't know what. All I know to do is take opportunities as they come and derive pleasure from them."

Dan cupped her chin with his hand and searched her eyes. "You're doing what is easiest for you and everybody. You're comfortable and want to perpetuate it."

"I like what I do."

"I know you do."

"There's nothing wrong with wanting to keep it."

"No there's not. So why are you unhappy?"

Her doubts flooded back. She took a guttural breath to ward away unwanted tears. "I don't know. It looks like I have everything." Her voice trembled as she went on. "Children love me. I like my work. I have devoted friends, an amorous fiancé that I'm about to marry."

Tears flowed, "But I'm confused. I thought I knew what I wanted. My life has progressed naturally. Who wouldn't want what I have?" Her shoulders convulsed as she tried to keep from crying aloud.

Dan put his arms around her and held her against his chest.

"What is this longing I'm feeling? What is that about?"

He held her silently, knowing she had to settle this within herself.

She imagined her life in Magdala and it was more of the same. She would never know adventure – would always be within the same box. She was caught in inertia, going around in a circle like a dreydl. She wanted her life to spiral upward, through endless possibilities.

Maybe she was just afraid to get married.

"Batia said this was just pre-wedding jitters, but I don't think my feelings are like other brides'."

"Maybe you like thinking you are needed."

"The girls need me."

"Yes, but you think you have to do everything. Have you ever given up control of the girls' club? Some things aren't yours to do."

"I delegate."

"True, but you're only satisfied if those you trust do things your way."

She stopped convulsing to look up at him. "That hurt."

And now she thought she could save the school by marrying Raamah. She didn't love him, but the end justified the means. As far as she was concerned, the school was more important than her own happiness. She was willing to make the sacrifice.

"Should I go back? Raamah might be worried."

"No, Raamah knows we need to pasture the flock until the full moon comes again."

They stayed in the Plain of Gennesaret for twelve more days and nights. They moved the flock out early on the thirteenth day, a day unlike the one when she had arrived.

The sky glowed soft and eerie over the far shore of the Sea of Galilee on their left. Maggie breathed deeply of the muted shades of alizarin illuminating the soft, wooly clouds. As they walked, the sun appeared coppery on the horizon, casting orange ink on a rippling silver sea.

~How great the sun's pure light! Only concerned with being; and sharing its beingness with the air, water, earth, and trees.~ The sky radiated joy in the glory of the sun.

CHAPTER 12

They arrived home in late afternoon. Powdery dust coated their feet and the hems of their tunics. The pungent odor of sheep and sweat permeated their clothing. That was the only thing Maggie didn't like about herding. She liked to be clean. She saw Sarina scurrying away with a group of girls.

Maggie stepped into the trough by the pen, held her breath, and lay down in the water. She wiggled in the cool liquid and ran her hands over her body to loosen the dirt from her skin. She arose with her tunic clinging to her form and rushed into the house to put on clean clothes. She would have a real bath after she and Dan ate and visited with the family. Later, she would go to the well for bath water and also replenish the trough where she had dipped.

Maggie embraced Edita in the kitchen. Edita readied the earthen tub for Maggie and pots of water boiled on the fire. Maggie took a pomegranate from the fruit bowl to assuage her hunger. Soon Dora appeared at the door. She had seen the flock from the market and hastened to Maggie's with scented oil for her bath.

The talk centered on the weather, the food, events in Magdala, and the terrain Maggie covered in her trip. No one asked why she left suddenly. She was a stray who wandered away and returned to the fold. They were just glad to see her.

It wasn't long before Sarina came back with girls carrying water. They filled the tub, expressed their joy at seeing her, and went away to give her privacy and resume their weaving. Edita poured hot water from the pots on the stove and Dora added jasmine to the mix. It was wonderful! Having sensitive, sharing, and considerate friends was better than having servants, she guessed. She might as well get used to it. When she was married to Raamah, she would learn how it felt to be waited on.

Would that make life better? She thought of Hannah with Zadika. They were best friends. Who would her servant be? Deborah? Lizette? Dora? One of the Girls? Or would Raamah, Eban, and Zadika choose a servant for her? She shuddered distastefully. The idea of ordering others around didn't appeal to her. Having friends to help her would be better. She didn't want to order them to perform the demeaning task of preparing her bath. ~Why me? Lizette would be better at this. She already has servants.~

She sighed. Raamah would know she had returned. How soon would he come to see her? How would he behave? She hoped she could have a good night's sleep before he came. She wanted to be rested when she saw him.

"Mama!"

Edita came into Maggie's bathing room, "What sweetie?"

"Do you think it would be all right to send one of the girls with a message to Raamah? I want to see him, but I want to wait until tomorrow."

"Good idea. That way, he won't come until you're ready. I'll send a couple of girls."

Satisfied she would be able to rest, she finished her bath and went to bed early. The household continued to bustle in the shop, Dan's wing, and the main part of the house.

Maggie was glad to be home. Her pilgrimage gave her a fresh perspective. Being away helped her view her life with wisdom born of detachment. She spent her next day visiting the club. After breakfast, the Second Years came to Enoch and Edita's to weave with Sarina. She helped Sarina for a while then went to Nanette and Jonathan's to see Janette plant potatoes with the Third Years. She dropped by the synagogue to see Lizette sing with the Fifth Years while Leora taught them a Yemenite dance.

Here she met Raamah who took her by the hand and spirited her away to the palace for lunch. There, the First Years did their first embroidery projects with Batia while Hannah and Zadika watched their every move. What a wonderful way for the seven-year-olds to learn patience, serenity, and confidence!

Raamah walked with her to Dora's where she and Deborah were busy with the Fourth Years, grinding herbs with mortar and pestle. She waved goodbye to Raamah and went home.

The late afternoon was a coming together to trace letters and words in the sand behind Enoch and Edita's. They picked up styluses whittled from strong twigs and wrote in prepared sand. The First Years wrote the beginning letters of words: cloth, thread, needle. The Second Years' words: loom, warp, woof, shuttle. The Third Years wrote sentences: I cut the eyes of the potatoes. I planted the eyes in the ground. I covered them with soil. I watered the plants. Fourth Years read dietary laws from Leviticus. Fifth Years took turns reading Psalms aloud while others wrote in clay.

The older girls grouped themselves in threes and took turns pitching, hitting, and catching. The younger ones chased balls and brought them back. The counselors and sponsors sat back and watched. There were now enough girls for a game. The older girls took their positions, some in the field and others in line for the stick. Maggie pitched for all of them during a quick game.

That evening, she walked with Raamah, "Did the girl's club go well without you?"

~Oh my God,~ thought Maggie, ~I hope he's not going back to his old sarcastic ways.~ She answered him evenly, "Of course it did. Sarina, Deborah, Janette, and Lizette are excellent at what they do. They have Mama, Leora, Batia, Nanette, Dora, Hannah, and Zadika to help them. What could go wrong? I wouldn't have taken the sheep to pasture if I didn't know it would go well without me."

There, she had defended herself without being defensive.

"I see you're very proud of your friends."

"Of course."

"Do you feel useless now that you know you aren't needed?"

What was he talking about?

"Not needed?"

"The club went a whole month without you and you said they did fine."

"Of course they did, but that doesn't mean I'm not needed."

"I see that I should have said that differently. You love them, they love you, and you won't want to give them up completely, but once we're married, you might not have time for them."

Maggie felt like she was slapped. She stared at him, repulsed, as if he were a serpent speaking to her from a tree in a garden. She wanted to turn and run.

"Raamah, I just remembered. I have a message for Dora." She left him hurriedly and went home.

Maggie wakened in her bed in the early morning hours. What would happen to the school if she wasn't there? Sarina, Deborah, Janette, and Lizette loved the school as much as she did. Together, they had all her abilities. Sarina could do everything she could except herd and play stickball. Everyone thought girls shouldn't do those things anyway. So no one would care if that wasn't done anymore, but they could still play.

The older girls could teach the younger. Giannella pitched very well and Gada was almost as good. Janette was great at telling stories, Lizette at singing ballads and psalms. Deborah understood gardening and herbal lore. Lizette had the personality to handle negotiations diplomatically.

If Maggie wasn't involved in the school, they would all step forward and apply their natural talents. Enoch and the older women were there to help out. Maggie was sure that all would be well if she were to drop off the face of the earth.

But where would she go? She could lead the sheep to green pastures far away. That's what most shepherds did. Few had acreage to graze locally like Enoch. She knew Enoch did it this way so he could have a family life and pursue his love of creating pottery. But he didn't want to give up the pastoral way of life and the closeness to nature that it lent.

And Raamah made that comment about her not needing to teach once they were married. He expected her to give up the club! He thought her sole purpose should be to tend him: to obey him, to fulfill his needs, to bed him, and to make him look good. He expected her to dissolve her own identity into his. Didn't he see that wasn't enough for Zadika? It couldn't be enough for her either. How could anyone be so dense and selfish?

Maggie loved Zadika. They had developed an understanding, reciprocal relationship. She knew Zadika approved of her marriage to her son. Zadika didn't see their marriage in the same way that Raamah did. Where Raamah thought Maggie would give up herself for him, Zadika thought Maggie would influence Raamah, make him more tolerant, less stringent, more flexible, less chauvinistic.

It was worth reflecting on that. Both those expectations were a prison of frustration. No. She couldn't sacrifice herself — not even for the club, and she couldn't change another person, particularly not Raamah. Zadika hadn't been able to raise him her way or to change him throughout the years. Eban's influence was irrevocable. After all, Raamah would be the next priest. Maggie would be stupid to think she could change hundreds of years of tradition.

She thought of Raamah's other option. ~Lizette!~

Lizette accepted the rules and ritual centered life of the Temple. She loved Raamah. She was committed to the school. Her feminine wiles and her desire to please him would influence Raamah to do things he never imagined. Lizette wouldn't resist his will, not like Maggie who would try to make him into something he wasn't. How miserable Maggie and Raamah would make each other!

Maggie's head ached from indecision. She dreaded the wedding, but it was inevitable. How could she let down her mother and shame her father? How could she disappoint her partners in the girls' club?

When she let Raamah have his way, it would be because it was her duty, not because she saw eye to eye with him.

Submission.

Compliance.

She threw the cover off and rolled over. She was attracted to Raamah. They shared a raw passion that would never be boring. His slick good looks were appealing. His prowess at stickball was a source of reluctant admiration to her, reluctant because he had inevitably been her opponent. He had an unfailing devotion to his mother. Would he adore her in the same way?

No, she didn't want that. He was condescending and indulgent to Zadika. That was a dishonest and backwards kind of love.

Ugh! He made her so angry!

Maggie grew cold as she considered breaking it off with him. What would she say?

~You don't love me? ~You want to change me? ~I care for you, but I want to change you?~

What would happen if she called it off?

He would be humiliated.

As she fretted over what to say, she conjured up his possible reactions. Would he fly in a rage, storm out, break things, or put an end to the girls' club? Each scenario was worse than the other.

She was still awake when a bird started singing outside. She wanted to roll over and sleep the sleep she had missed during the night.

But she had to get up. It was her turn to take out the sheep!

When she reached the road, Raamah was there, waiting with a tall, strong servant.

She had never thought he would go with her to the fields. This was a new idea to her. She had often herded with Dan, and on occasion, her sisters. She herded with Jesus when they were young. She never thought of herding with Raamah. She supposed he brought the servant along to carry things.

She continued walking, expecting him to join her. He called her back while the servant walked with the herd.

She went to him, oblivious that he was repulsed by her boy's clothing. "I'm so glad you're going to join me with the flock today. I wish I had known you were coming. I would have brought the balls and sticks." She walked as she talked and he had to follow her. "We could hit balls while the sheep are grazing.

"But that's okay. We can do that another day. I brought my embroidery and my harp. We can sing together. I have a slingshot for target practice."

He grew agitated, "Maggie, I'm not here to herd with you."

Puzzled, she stopped in the middle of the road. The flock went around her. "Why are you here?"

"I came to take you back. Allan will herd your sheep from now on."

"Allan? Herd my sheep? He doesn't know my sheep. He doesn't know our signals. The dogs won't answer to him."

"Look at him. He's doing fine."

"That's because I'm here. He doesn't know our pastures."

He took part of her load and grabbed her hand, "Then he'll herd them in the temple pastures. We'll send Dan to help him." He led her back toward the village.

She pulled back. "Dan's running the shop today."

He overcame her resistance, putting his arm under hers so she would have to walk beside him.

Maggie was outraged, "People are staring. You're causing a scene."

"It's you who are causing a scene. Come with me."

She fumed, "Are you going to take away everything I love?"

"Grow up, Maggie."

"Grow up? What makes you think I'm not grown?"

"Grown women don't herd sheep and play stickball. They don't do target practice with slingshots."

Maggie was nonplussed, "Dan is grown and he herds and plays ball and uses a slingshot. You play ball. Even you."

"But we're men."

"Oh! So, just because I'm a woman, I have to give those things up?"

"You're not just any woman. You are betrothed to the next priest. You have a position to fill. You can't be a laughing stock."

"Then why me? Why don't you marry someone else?"

"Maggie," he said warningly.

She tromped into her house.

Raamah threw up his hands in disbelief.

No one was home. Her first thought was about the sheep. They were her responsibility today. She was sure Allan was a competent shepherd. Raamah would not have appointed someone who was not, but the flock would be confused. Bo and Abbe would feel abandoned. It takes a while to grow trust with animals.

Surreptitiously, she looked out the window in hopes Raamah was gone. She had to get back to the flock, but he was there, pacing back and forth. How was she going to get past him? She could sneak out the back and walk along the sea until she got out of town, but he would see her. He would only have to look. There was nothing to hide behind.

What would she do if it wasn't her day to herd? She'd be with Dora or the girls. The girls were at Dora's today! She changed into her feminine garb and put her boy's clothes in a basket with her lunch, slingshot, and embroidery.

She made an ostentatious display of walking out of the house and passing Raamah. She turned toward Dora's, thankful it was on her way to the fields. He joined her determined footsteps, "I see you've come to your senses. You're dressed appropriately."

She turned on him, "Now you're dictating how I dress?"

"Maggie," he said reasonably, "A priest's wife can't wear a boy's costume." He was a priest. He would know what it said in

Deuteronomy about women wearing men's clothing and men wearing women's apparel.

"She can if she's going to herd sheep!"

"She can't herd sheep!"

"Certainly not in her best clothes!"

"Leave me alone now. I'm going to help the girls gather seeds at Dora's." She walked toward Dora's.

She was relieved when he stopped in his tracks, frustrated, his dignity intact.

~Who does he think he is, telling me what not to do, how not to dress?~

Not daring to look back, she kept her determined pace all the way to Dora's. She wished she had eyes in back of her head so she could be sure he wasn't following her. As soon as she turned off the street to go up Dora's front path, she turned her head toward the girls, but peeled her eyes to see if he was on the road.

Convinced he hadn't followed, she rushed to the back shed, hastily changed into her herding clothes, and escaped out the back street. She placed herself in front of a donkey pulling a wagon and blended in with others going about their business.

She walked as fast as she could. She dared not run. That would attract attention and someone might recognize her and tell Raamah.

Disturbed by the delay and concerned that she might not catch up with the flock, she took comfort that it couldn't move faster than the smallest lamb. Coming to the end of the back road, she turned toward the main one and looked back to be sure that Raamah wasn't coming. Seeing the way clear, she found the dusty mixture of sheep, dog, and man tracks. She could follow them easily until they turned off the road, then she would know what direction they went.

She approached the herd, confident Raamah wouldn't find her. He was clueless about herding and wouldn't know where to look.

The sheep were unsettled. Few grazed and most moved about restlessly. Groups headed many directions. The lambs wandered among the ewes. Bo and Abbe were confused. Allan wasn't any more assured than the animals. There was no respect.

He ran to position himself on the far side of the strays then shouted, waving his hands, hoping to drive them back to the flock. They just looked at him as if he were speaking a strange language, and went past him, even further away from the flock.

Maggie would have laughed if it hadn't been so pathetic. This was the reason shepherds should know their sheep. There were two approaches to herding sheep, her father's way, and the wrong way. Her father had the sheep come to him and led them. Foolish shepherds got behind the sheep and drove them away from them.

No wonder Allan couldn't handle this flock. The crazy-man scenario meant nothing to them.

She allowed herself to watch the groups of sheep scatter over the countryside. Bo and Abbe spotted her and came to sit on their haunches and look up at her curiously, shifting their feet and whining. As far as she could tell, Allan hadn't seen her. Maybe he didn't know how to handle dogs. He hadn't set the boundaries for the flock and the dogs didn't know what to do.

~I don't think I would like herding if I tried to do it his way.~ She gave the gathering call, a seductive whistle that wove up and down like thread through cloth. The sheep stilled and listened. She walked toward Raphaela who was now the leader of the herd, continuing the tones until they formed a compact mass of four-legged-wooly bodies, and then she walked around them giving them a wide berth of freedom to rest, play, and graze. The dogs settled on the outside of the perimeter she set.

Allan came to her, astonished, "I didn't know how glad I could be to see someone." She led him to a vantage point where they could watch the flock.

She decided it might be good to have another shepherd to work Enoch's flock. She supposed Allan could learn. He'd already formed the appropriate conclusion from his first lesson: His way didn't work!

"Excuse me for a minute while I calm the flock." She hadn't brought her harp. It was too big to hide under her clothing and would have given away her intention of returning to the sheep when she went by Raamah. She pulled out her reed flute and intoned a melancholy tune. The flock applied themselves to their grazing. Some lay on their side and chewed their cud. When she was satisfied her music had its desired effect, she conferred with Allan.

They talked of the sheep, their personalities and dispositions: that Raphaela had grown from an injured lamb to her position as lead, the dogs' duty to establish the boundaries, showing them the layout for the day, how to gather the sheep, and lead them. He wasn't accustomed to using music in the way that she had learned with

Enoch and Dan. She gave him the flute to play with until he could produce a calming effect. The gathering whistle wasn't very difficult. He caught on quickly. She helped him establish himself with Bo and Abbe and coached him on a few simple commands.

He looked at her with respect, "It must be true."

"What's that?"

"It's true that you killed a wolf that was after your sheep, isn't it?"

She stilled herself. She didn't think anyone knew about that.

He saw the concern in her face. "It's okay. I won't tell Raamah. Only the shepherds know."

She was slightly relieved, but if the shepherds knew, what would keep Raamah from finding out?

He hastened to assure her, "I didn't even know it was you. I just knew it was a shepherdess who killed that wolf a few years ago. There are not many girls who herd. It would almost have to be you."

"Now it makes sense. You have control over the herd. Someone with less skill would have lost their flock while going after the wolf."

Maggie neither refuted nor affirmed his supposition. After a few rounds of target practice she was satisfied that he handled a slingshot well. What did he know about tending injuries? She showed him her medicine pouch and talked about which ones to use for different situations.

As they led the flock home, she showed him Dora's hut where he could take animals with serious injuries. She halted the flock to introduce him to Dora and sent him the rest of the way to Enoch's with the flock.

She changed her clothes in Dora's shed and poured water over her body. She stayed at Dora's until she thought it was safe to go back home.

Dora poured tea. She wanted to hear everything, "You came and went this morning like a phantom. What was that all about?"

"I just learned why I'm a good shepherd."

"Do tell."

Maggie told Dora of the events of the day and introducing Allan to the sheep.

"So you marry Raamah and Allan takes your place with the sheep."

"That's what he wants."

Dora raised her eyebrows meaningfully over her tea cup, "Is that what you want?"

"I think it's inevitable." Maggie sipped thoughtfully. "I don't want to give up herding, but I will have more to do when I get married and move to the palace. Papa and Dan need help. I can't take my turn as often. If Allan goes out with each of us, he will eventually be a good herdsman. Raamah mentioned letting our flock pasture on Temple lands."

Dora frowned, "Will Enoch allow that?"

"I guess he'll work that out with Eban one way or another." Maggie shrugged, "It could be part of the marriage agreement. She carried her cup to the window to stare at Dora's garden. "Raamah's making demands. He says I'll have to give up stickball."

"How do you feel about that?"

"I guess I'd have to give up playing stickball anyway, but I'm really angry that he's forcing me."

"You don't even force your sheep. It sounds like Raamah needs to take herding lessons."

"True, I wonder if we can make his herding lessons part of the marriage agreement," She gave a dry laugh. "He says I have to give up the girls' club?"

"Why does he want you to do that?"

"I think it's a power play. I won't give up the girls' club. Can't he see how much it helps girls?" She sat across from Dora. "In fact, I want us to expand it. I want us to start a girls' school in the palace."

Dora liked the idea, "That would be such a wonderful thing."

"We could have our classes there and play on the grounds. I'm sure Zadika would love it."

"You think Eban and Raamah would agree to that?"

"They'll want to please their wives."

Dora sighed, "Maggie."

"What?"

"You can't count on Eban and Raamah doing that."

"Why not? Mama got Papa to help with the girls' club. I can get Raamah to do the same thing. We'll be married."

"Not all men are as reasonable as Enoch. Has Raamah told you he'll support the girls' club?"

Maggie averted her eyes and rose from her seat to wipe the shelves. "Zadika got Eban to let us keep it."

"Maggie?"

"No, Raamah hasn't said he'd approve of the girls' club. He wants me to stop doing the girls' club."

Dora let that sink in. She wiped each bottle and replaced them on the shelves. "You've accomplished a lot you can be proud of and now you're betrothed to a fine man. What do you like most about him?"

"He's crazy in love with me and sure that I'm the one for him. I like that – even when I frustrate him like I did today."

"You think he'll eventually get tired of being frustrated and give in?"

"To a certain extent. I gave in enough to accept help with the herding."

"Could you have done that without drama this morning?"

"I didn't think so at the time."

"You will have to maintain your dignity around your servants."

"I think we did that today. Allan went on and missed our argument. When I found him later, I instructed him."

"I'd say you did well with your first servant encounter." She rinsed her rag in the basin. "How could you have accepted the help and then instructed Allan with Raamah's cooperation?"

"The best thing would have been for Raamah to go out in the field with us."

"That's what you expected him to do at first."

"And he was determined not to go. He even pulled me the other way so I couldn't."

"The two of you could have discussed it and reasoned it out together. He's an intelligent man. He'd understand that Allan needed instruction."

"You'd think so, but I didn't realize how much until I saw him with the herd. I knew Papa was a different kind of shepherd, I just didn't know how different. I expected Allan to be competent since Raamah appointed him."

"So why were you determined to get back to the flock?"

"Because they were my responsibility."

"Is that the real reason? Think about it, Maggie."

165

Maggie checked the contents of the comfrey vial. "I wanted to get back because Raamah forced me to stay away." She set it aside, "There, I said it."

Dora leaned on the high working table. "I think you would be willing to cooperate if he talked to you about it first. Then you could have agreed to try it as a compromise."

"There would be less turmoil that way."

"But he's in love with you."

Dora cleared another shelf and Maggie wiped it clean.

"What else do you like about Raamah?"

"He's good looking when he looks at me in that intense way he has."

"So you have passion. That's a nice thing to have in a marriage, if you use it for love instead of anger. You'll have to be patient with him so you can teach him."

"Teach him?"

"Like a child. He didn't learn the same things you did in childhood and you didn't learn what he did. You need to learn from each other."

"So I teach him instead of getting angry."

"You accept him as he is, then teach him. He loves you. He'll learn if you do it lovingly." She looked at Maggie affectionately. "Like the girls. You don't expect the girls to already know everything. You can't expect him to either."

They had cleaned half the shelves by now.

"What else do you like about Raamah?"

"He's rich."

"That never hurts. Is that why you're marrying him?"

"I'm marrying him because Papa betrothed me to him."

"Not really. You could have refused. What's in this for you?"

"I'll live in the palace."

"That's not the sort of thing that impresses you."

"It will put me in position to easily help and heal people. I can use the palace to form a girls' school. Raamah will get the elders to support it."

Dora put down her towel, took Maggie hands in her own, and looked into her bright, beautiful eyes. "Those are wonderful aspirations, Maggie. I want only the best for you and I know you'll have it." She hugged her and held her. Neither wanted to let go and they stood, clinging to each other, letting their love sink in,

That evening, Dora sat under the acacia in her garden with her fingers wrapped around a warm cup of chamomile.

~Destiny is an interesting thing. It's hidden over, under, around, and above the thin robe of earth that we take for this life. Such an ephemeral robe, but its fiber clings so closely that we don't know what we are really about.

~This course of events has Maggie on the verge of marrying Raamah. If that is what is to be, let it be.~

The sense of dread Dora felt over the marriage was irrefutable.

~How much of Maggie will be lost in this marriage? In the palace? Maggie's enthusiasm and zest for life are contagious and irrepressible. Everyone wants to help Maggie because she always does enticing and energetic things. She is a great leader, exactly what is needed in a priest's wife. I can see why Raamah wants her.

~Let it be.

~It can only benefit Magdala, but what about Maggie? ~

She thought about the lessons Maggie would learn.

~She will have to stand firm against repression from temple traditions. She will have to support Raamah and expand his view. Won't he be astounded when his duties reap far more than he expects because she's involved? The women will be drawn to her. She'll include them and they'll love their lives. The men will grow in their being.

~If this marriage is what Maggie chooses to accept, all will be better for it.~

In the family barn, milking Elsie, Maggie saw another point of view.

~If I don't marry Raamah, what will I do? I'll never find anyone else. I'm not attracted to anyone. I'll help Dora heal. I'll herd. Allan can go back to the Temple flock. I'll do the girls' club. ~

It all seemed pointless and mundane when compared with the possibilities of palace life. And someone else would take her place beside Raamah.

But no one would do it like she could.

CHAPTER 13

Maggie was among the women, preparing for her wedding. She was freshly bathed and combed her hair, using Dora's herbs to put a light scent in her auburn tresses. The girls talked about the guests. Leora said that Joseph of Nazareth would be here as he was in town for a building job.

Maggie felt an inner urge. Her heart surged and her imagination soared. Was this her answer? Not wanting to give herself away, she gingerly resumed her combing. "I guess Jesus came to work with him," she said to Leora.

"Lands, no! He took off for the Far East a few years ago, soon after he came of age."

Maggie put down her comb. "How long have you known this?"

"Oh, I just found out yesterday when Samuel asked Joseph about him."

"Didn't we get word that Jesus married that rich merchant's daughter four or five years ago?"

"Apparently it was only a rumor. Rebecca pursued him persistently the year after he came of age, hoping to be betrothed to him. He resisted her suit and left on a journey to India with Prince Ravanna of Orissa."

"I thought he stopped coming to Magdala because he was married."

"It's amazing how gossip can distort the truth."

"Has Rebecca married someone else?"

"They say she refuses suitors hoping he'll come back."

Maggie thoughtfully took up her pot of oil to rub her body with the essence of rose. Then put it back. Suddenly the strong scents were repugnant. Her sisters, Deborah, and the other women were braiding each other's hair.

She was seized with a longing for the days when she played by the Sea of Galilee with Jesus. She measured all her friendships by the one she had with him. His imaginative play. His closeness to nature. His understanding of the spiritual nature of people. She never thought of him as a potential suitor. He was only a good friend. They hadn't restrict their conversations to appropriate subjects between male and female. No subject was taboo. There had been no barriers between them, just an open, friendly relationship.

She knew she would never have that with Raamah. She braided her hair thoughtfully, barely aware of the activity around her. Raamah had admired her, from a distance, except for stickball. He and Izaak taunted her mercilessly when she pitched. She and he were invariably on opposite teams when they chose sides since they were the two best players.

After she had come of age, it was frowned on for her to play with the boys. Boys and girls were separated at synagogue, festival, and social occasions. Maggie longed for the old days when they were children and all played together. Now, she had no male friends, unless you could count her brother, Dan, but he was ten years older and married with his own household. Now she saw more of his wife, Batia, than she did him.

She thought how difficult it was to know men because of rigidly defined gender roles. The women were together, cooking, sewing, and cleaning. The men were together fishing, building, and tending animals.

She would be running Raamah's home, not even cooking, cleaning, and mending. All for a man she didn't love. Oh, he had a great reputation in Magdala because of his stickball prowess, but he was never sensitive to her. He wanted her for a wife because she was attractive, from a good family, but he didn't know her. His mother entered the room. Zadika lacked the energetic persona extended by the women in Maggie's family. She was somewhat withdrawn, as if afraid and didn't speak unless spoken to. She wondered what kind of husband Raamah's father must be for his wife to be such a fawning creature. Looking at the woman, Maggie knew she didn't want to go through with the wedding. She would not allow her spirit to be tread upon!

She caught Dora's eyes, "Dora, would you help the ladies select their scents?"

She slipped out of the room, ostensibly to be alone, as Dora opened her herbal pouch and displayed selections of scented oils.

Maggie rushed out of the side of the synagogue away from the gathering crowd. She took a back street to avoid the courtyard and hurried home.

In the room she shared with Sarina, she threw off her wedding paraphernalia and gathered her belongings. She hadn't realized she had so little that would be of use on a long journey. She had never been farther than Jerusalem at Passover. Frustrated, she went to Daniel's room and donned a yarmulke, one of his tunics, and a light robe then put one of his older tunics in a bag.

Thinking it would be cold in India; she grabbed one of his heavier robes and took his toughest boots. They were too big, but they would have to do. She would wrap some rags around her feet to make them fit snugly. She started to take one of his sheepskins but had a better idea. Going back to her room, she unearthed the much loved but unused wolf pelt from under her bed. What a wonderful thing to take on an adventure!

She rushed to Dora's cottage. She trusted Dora. She could depend on her to help. She rummaged in Dora's pantry.

Dora entered soon after Maggie walked in the door. She wasn't surprised to see Maggie. "I noticed how disturbed you were. I thought I would find you here." She saw Maggie's boy's clothes and smiled at the appearance of the wolf hide, knowing what it meant to her. She went to the cupboard. "I took as long as I could to give the ladies their perfumed oils." She wrapped some loaves and fishes in a heavy cloth and handed them to Maggie. "Where are you going?"

"I'm going to find Jesus. Dora, Leora said he isn't married. He went to study in the Far East. I'm going to find him. I'll be gone a long time and before I get back, this crazy idea of marriage to Raamah will blow over. He will find someone else and Father will give up on the idea."

"You realize that Enoch will have to disown you. He will lose face and Raamah will be humiliated."

"But that's better than marriage to Raamah. He can be cruel and spiteful. Find a way to get him to marry Lizette."

Dora knew better than to argue. She had no right to do anything that would alter Maggie's destiny even though it tore her heart to watch her go. "As long as you've thought this through. Hurry on then. I'll cover for you with Edita. I'll let them worry a few days to give you time to get down the road. It'll be too late for them to find you when I let them know you're in good hands with Jesus.

As soon as Maggie left, Dora packed a bag with supplies and went to hide in a cave until the time was right.

Okay! How dramatic can it get?

A runaway bride. It's happened before and it happens again. Remember the movie about it in 1999.

Maybe the Magdalene borrowed from that.

Or vice versa.

It's chickens and eggs. No one knows what came first.

But we're ascended ones with accesses to the collective intelligence of the Akashic records[1]. We know everything happens at the same time. There is no past or future, only an eternal present. That which is called time is not linear. Nothing can happen before anything else. It's like a cosmic chord.

That can never be lost.

This will put a new slant on things and alter past events in the future.

Alter them?

Two thousand years from now, someone will discover it and make it known.

Are you sure?

Positively. I see it in a glimmer from the higher frequencies.

Aaah. Now I see it too. The sun of God that alters the past to change the future.

Let it be.

Let's pass into the alternate universe that the sun is making.

They focused on the glimmering portal of light until it permeated their consciousnesses and surrounded their sphere of influence in a soft glow.

This is definitely different . . . freer somehow.

We can finish the curriculum from here.

The holographic pattern is a higher frequency.

The earth illusion will continue to adjust.

That will take at least two thousand years.

Lasting change only occurs gradually in this Piscean Era.

But not in the time to come. Things can alter instantly in the Aquarian vibration.

Even more quickly after the adjustment to this alternate reality

---

[1] Information, desires, and experiences recorded on the ethers that interpenetrate and surround all things. The Book of Life. The aggregation of the thought-forms of every human unit throughout time that are encoded in a non-physical plane of existence known as the astral plane.

Coming Soon

robe of earth

A spiritual fantasy
Of the legendary
Mary of Magdala:

Book Two

by Flossie Jordan

APPENDIX

GLOSSARY OF NAMES

Aaron – mountain, boy in Magdala, plays stickball with Maggie

Abbe – rejoicing, sheep dog

Andra – one of the twelve maidens at Mount Carmel

Archaii Faith – Archaii of first ray of faith, embodied as the disciple Peter

Archangel Gabriel – Archangel of the fifth ray to our Earth representing truth, science, healing, concentration, and consecration.

Barak – flash of light, boy in Magdala, plays stickball with Maggie

Batia – daughter of God; Leora's best friend, Dan's wife, Maggie's sister-in-law

Bessie – my God is a vow, old ewe and head of the flock

Bo – handsome, sheep dog

Carmine – garden, orchard; Raamah's friend

Chanda – God and compassion; young girl in Magdala

Dan – arbiter, brother to Mary Magdalene

Deborah – bee, young Maggie's best friend, daughter of Jonathan and Nanette, sister to Janette and Samuel, Jesus' cousin

Diana – one of the twelve maidens at Mount Carmel

Dora – Mary Magdalene's mentor, wise woman and healer

Dwahl Kuhl – master of the second ray of enlightenment; embodied as one of the three Wise Men

Eban – stone, Raamah's father; Zadika's husband; priest of Magdala

Ebilina – woman who had a child in Magdala

Edita – mother of Dan, Leora, Sarina, and Mary Magdalene; wife to Enoch; daughter to innkeeper Apsophar and Sadaphe; one of the twelve maidens at Mount Carmel; present at Jesus' birth

El Morya – Chohan of the first ray of divine will, power, and faith; embodied as one of the three Wise Men

Elijah – embodied as John the Baptist

Ella – Ebilina's mother in Magdala

Elsie – my God is a vow – milk goat

Enoch – devoted dedicated; Essene man; father of Dan, Leora, Sarina, and Mary Magdalene; husband to Edita

Enosh – man, boy in Magdala, plays stickball with Maggie

Hannah – Zadika's handmaiden

Hosea – to deliver

Ian – God is forgiving,

Izaak – he will laugh, Raamah's best friend

Janette – daughter to Jonathan and Nanette, sister to Samuel and Deborah, Jesus' cousin

Jesus – childhood friend of Maggie's, Essene boy from Nazareth

Joanna – one of the twelve maidens at Mount Carmel

Jonathan – Essene man; best friend of Enoch; father to Deborah, Janette, and Samuel; Mother Mary's fisherman brother in Magdala, Jesus' uncle

Josada – one of the twelve maidens at Mount Carmel

Joseph – Jesus' father, a carpenter in Nazareth, Essene man

Josie – one of the twelve maidens at Mount Carmel

Judy – teacher at Mount Carmel, Archaii Constance of the second ray of constancy

Karmic Board – a committee to plan earth's redemption

Kuthumi – Chohan of the second ray of illumination, wisdom, and understanding; embodied as one of the three Wise Men

Kwan Yin – Master of the seventh ray of mercy, compassion, forgiveness, and exemplary family life; Mary Magdalene's guardian and guide

Leora – my light, sister to Mary Magdalene

Lizette – my god is a vow, one of young Maggie's best friends

Margil – one of the twelve maidens at Mount Carmel, midwife at Jesus birth

Martha – Lazarus and Young Mary's sister in Bethany

Mary – Jesus' mother, one of twelve maiden's at Mount Carmel

Micah – Angel of Unity in charge of the Piscean Age who embodied as Jesus, Divine Complement to Lady Nada

Miriam – one of the twelve maidens at Mount Carmel

Mother Mary – Archaii of the fifth ray of the Immaculate Concept who embodied to birth and nurture Jesus; one of the twelve maidens at Mount Carmel

Nada – Lady Master of the sixth ray of ministration, peace, and grace; embodied as Mary Magdalene; Divine Complement to Jesus

Nanette – grace, favor, one of the twelve maidens at Mount Carmel; best friend to Edita; mother of Deborah, Janette, and Samuel, wife of Jonathan

Raamah – thunder, priest's son in Magdala, betrothed to Maggie

Raphaela – God has healed, rescued lamb, later head of the flock

Saint Germain – Chohan of the seventh ray of transmutation and freedom, embodied as Joseph father of Jesus

Salome – peace; mother of James, John, David, Naomi; wife to Zebedee; one of the twelve maidens at Mount Carmel

Samuel – his name is God, Jonathan and Nanette's son, Janette and Deborah's brother, Leora's husband, Magdalena's brother-in-law, Jesus' cousin

Sanat Kumara was Lord of the World who came from Venus to save Earth

Saraphe – sister to Edita, aunt to Mary Magdalene, daughter to innkeeper Apsaphar and Sadaphe, present at Jesus' birth and first to hold Jesus

Sarina – princess, sister to Mary Magdalene

Sophi – one of the twelve maidens at Mount Carmel

Suzanna – one of the twelve maidens at Mount Carmel

Tobias – God is good, boy in Magdala, played stickball with young Maggie

Ximena – listening; young girl in Magdala

Yaar – woodland, forest; apprentice to Enoch, played stickball with young Maggie, marries Deborah

Young Mary – Lazarus and Martha's sister

Zadika – righteous, just; Raamah's mother; Priest Eban's wife in Magdala

Zebedee – father of James, John, David, Naomi; husband to Salome

PUBLICATIONS

The following publications were used as inspiration for Book One of
robe of earth:

Bridge to Freedom publications. Kings Park, Long Island, NY.

Dowling, Levi, scribe. (1907) *The Aquarian Gospel of Jesus the Christ*, DeVorss & Co., Marina Del Rey, CA.

Edman, Irwin, editor. (1956) *The Works of Plato*, Random House, NY.

Foundation for Inner Peace. (1975) *A Course in Miracles*, Foundation for Inner Peace, Glen Ellen, CA.

Furst, Jeffrey, editor. (1968) *Edgar Cayce's Story of Jesus*, Coward-McCann, Inc. NY.

Lamsa, George M., translator. (1933) *Holy Bible: from the Ancient Eastern Text*, Harper Collins Publishers, NY.

Michener, James A. (1965) *The Source*. Random House, NY.

Papastavro, Tellis S. (1972) *The Gnosis and the Law*, New Age Study of Humanity's Purpose, Tucson, AZ.

Spalding, Baird T. (1935) *Life and Teaching of the Masters of the Far East*, DeVorss & Co., Marina Del Rey, CA.

Székely, Edmond B. translator and editor. (1981) *The Essene Gospel of Peace, Book One: Lost Scrolls of the Essene Brotherhood*, International Biogenic Society, Matsqui, BC, Canada.

Urantia Foundation. (1955) *The Urantia Book*, Urantia Foundation, Chicago, IL.

Made in the USA
Middletown, DE
06 October 2020